THE
GRACE
WITHIN

CRISTA SALVATORE

Halo Publishing International
8000 W Interstate 10, #600
San Antonio, Texas 78230

First Edition, February 2023
Printed in the United States of America
ISBN: 978-1-63765-276-3
Library of Congress Control Number: 2022913498

The information contained within this book is strictly for informational purposes. Unless otherwise indicated, all the names, characters, businesses, places, events and incidents in this book are either the product of the author's imagination or used in a fictitious manner. Any resemblance to actual persons, living or dead, or actual events is purely coincidental.

Halo Publishing International is a self-publishing company that publishes adult fiction and non-fiction, children's literature, self-help, spiritual, and faith-based books. We continually strive to help authors reach their publishing goals and provide many different services that help them do so. We do not publish books that are deemed to be politically, religiously, or socially disrespectful, or books that are sexually provocative, including erotica. Halo reserves the right to refuse publication of any manuscript if it is deemed not to be in line with our principles. Do you have a book idea you would like us to consider publishing? Please visit www.halopublishing.com for more information.

Disclaimer

Neither the author or publisher, nor any authors, contributors, or other representatives will be liable for damages arising out of or in connection with the use of this book. This is a comprehensive limitation of liability that applies to all damages of any kind, including (without limitation) compensatory; direct, indirect or consequential damages; loss of data, income or profit; loss of or damage to property and claims of third parties.

You understand that this book is not intended as a substitute for consultation with a licensed healthcare practitioner, such as your physician. Before you begin any healthcare program, or change your lifestyle in any way, you will consult your physician or another licensed healthcare practitioner to ensure that you are in good health.

This book provides content related to physical and/or mental health issues. As such, use of this book implies your acceptance of this disclaimer.

The information presented is the author's opinion and does not constitute any health or medical advice. The content of this book is for entertainment purposes only and is not intended to diagnose, treat, cure, or prevent any condition or disease.

This book is not intended as a substitute for the medical advice of physicians. The author is not a licensed therapist. The reader should regularly consult a therapist in matters relating to his/her health and particularly with respect to any symptoms that may require diagnosis or medical attention.

To my mom and dad, for encouraging my creativity by signing me up for a summer writing class when I was ten years old. Thank you for believing in me.

For anyone who is brave enough to love again, even after a broken heart.

Contents

Preface

Dear Reader,

My intentions for writing this book were:

1. To fulfill the desire, deep down, to write a book.

2. To have fun expressing my creativity through fiction.

3. Most of all, to spark insight and healing within everyone who reads it.

My philosophy is that we are not meant to be alone. At the core of it all, we as human beings crave connection and love. The people in our lives teach us about ourselves and how we operate in the world. Relationships, especially the intimate ones, are the major contributors to our lives. They mirror what is going on inside of us, even though we may not always recognize it. They lift us up and break us down; they open us and close us; they excite us and challenge us.

This book has been an idea within me for a long time. It is written as a parable, a story from which you may learn. You may recognize yourself or your best friend in the pages that follow. The beauty is that each person learns something different as the story unfolds.

My hope is that people can relate to the characters, their trials, and their triumphs. I wish I could say that I have figured it out, but the truth is, I'm still working on it. Some days I feel I have moved a bit forward, and then others I am back to square one. I am still deepening my ability to love others and myself.

As you embark on the journey with Grace, I invite you to be as open as possible, answer the questions and complete the activities at the end of each chapter. It is a time for self-reflection or conversations with close friends, partners, or even book clubs. You will have the opportunity to deepen the connection you have with yourself. The time you spend with yourself is worth it because you are worth it.

I've written this with an open heart, and in so doing, I have gained insights into myself. Sharing it with the world enabled me to be more vulnerable and brave with my own self-expression and voice.

I am thankful for all the twists and turns in my love life along the way. The anger and sadness hid the silver lining when my relationships did not go according to my plan. I now see that those emotions played a part in my growth, and I walked away with more clarity, even if it was painful. Each time I open my heart, I am one step closer to being true to myself and connecting more in my relationships.

Thank you for making space in your life for this book. My hope is that you continue to grow and transform because of the people with whom you surround yourself, especially those who are the closest. Be brave. Be open to love. Be YOU.

With gratitude and love,

Crista

Chapter 1

Grace

Not again. I think to myself. It is as though it's Groundhog Day, and not a day you want to keep reliving. In this case, it was having the same conversation, different guy. I was sure that it was going to work out. Thinking about the failure causes me to have a pit in my stomach. The day was a bit of a waste, couldn't concentrate at work. I did my best to avoid fellow colleagues as much as I could, to be stoic and not let people know I was upset, but I doubt I pulled it off. I barely ate and just stared at my screen. I hated the fact that this was getting in the way of my work, which for the most part I enjoyed. Maybe the pit was from having only one bagel and two Americanos from the Bluestone Lane Café, swimming in my stomach that day. It was odd for me not to have an appetite because I love food and appreciate all the options that are right outside my door.

The barista was perplexed when I entered through the doorway for a second visit at four o'clock. I am usually a once-a-day kind of coffee drinker, trying to be somewhat conscious of my caffeine intake. Although I never refuse a quality cup of coffee. But at that point I did not care. Caffeine was my friend; it helped me to numb the pain. Every time I took a sip, it was a distraction and a sure way to swallow my deep sadness brought on by another failed relationship. My pain was endless, and my heart was broken. I knew it was beyond my ability to bury my emotions and stuff them deep down so that I did not have to deal with them. I was an emotional, ticking time bomb, and I was barely keeping the explosion contained. I did not know whether I would scream or cry; neither option would be appropriate in public.

I looked around at the office workers and locals laughing and conversing over their espressos. It annoyed me how everyone in the coffee shop seemed so happy. I hated happy that afternoon. I wanted everyone to be as miserable as I was.

It is finally go time—six thirty as I approach a different coffee shop. I would dare not enter my Bluestone Lane. Let's face it; my barista would think I was crazytown ordering yet another shot of finely made jolt. I really like the way he always greets me with a smile and knows my name by heart. At this vulnerable moment, the last thing I need is to be judged by him or anyone. Plus, he has perfected my Americano by diluting not one but two espresso shots with hot water, giving it an extra kick. I also love the vibe of the place and don't want the breakup to taint the good energy I feel every time I walk in. Derrick mentioned meeting at a Starbucks where we will say our goodbyes and exchange toiletries left at each other's apartment. We will meet for our relationship's last episode, or shall we say our grand finale.

I decided to get my hair blown out at the local Drybar for the occasion. People may mock me or even think I am crazy to take such care with my appearance for an unhappy event. But I seriously don't care what anyone thinks right now (except perhaps for my favorite barista). I am in an emotional survival zone. Most people went for blowouts for special occasions, like birthdays, an important interview, or even a big date. Not me. One thing for sure is that I am going down in style. I usually chose the Straight Up—simple with a touch of body. Not a lot of fanfare or even product needed, but an enhancement of my natural beauty. Deep down, I want him to know what he is going to be missing.

I chose one of my favorite Ted Baker London dresses—the perfect combination of professional and feminine. The bold blue complements my skin tone, and the subtle houndstooth print whispers sophistication, inspiring strangers to compliment me as I walk down the street. It is my favorite brand, although I know I have to watch my spending. This is no Ann Taylor off the sale rack. It was a reality check when I gave the sales associate my credit card and saw the total right above the dotted line; I made the promise to shell out a pretty penny for this dress. Anytime I want to justify a splurge, I ask myself, *Can you ever put a price on feeling beautiful and powerful?* Knowing my truth made me buy the dress. When the bill came, I had a bit of buyer's remorse as I withdrew the funds from my bank account. That feeling dissipates, though, every time I see myself in the mirror. It is the same routine every time I wear this dress. I spin around, the breeze causing the dress to flow all around me. I smile as I admire the waist-defining sash. I feel good in it, and this afternoon I welcomed anything that would boost my self-esteem.

If I shared my exit strategy with my friends, they would say, "Why waste a perfectly good dress and blowout on him?" Except for Hope. I am sure she would get it. It is not for him; it is for me. It helps me retain that one ounce of dignity by leaving on Grace's terms.

Finally, on what feels like the longest day of my life, I walk through the door of the café, and I take a deep breath. *Let's get this over with and rip off the bandage. Quick and painless.* But who am I kidding? Nothing about this is quick, and it certainly isn't painless. It is unbelievably hurtful and devastating.

Derrick and I have dated for three years. It doesn't seem like a long time, but I fell hard and quickly. For me, it was a big deal. My heart's investment was large. I am forty-two, and he is the first man I ever really wanted to marry.

Most of my friends already have two-point-five kids and live in the burbs. I play the tough, contented, single career woman, but secretly I pictured my life turning out like that of my friends. No such luck, and it was not as though I haven't tried. I have dated many men, but every one of them has come up short. At times I have been set up by someone, gone out with friends, gone on numerous dating apps, and even invested in a matchmaker. The entire process is exhausting and quite discouraging. My attitude could be better about it. I'm not like my friend Hope; she is much more relaxed and open. I am completely closed off when I go out these days, but don't realize it until I debrief the date with Hope. By that time, it's too late.

I have stubbornly resisted opening my heart, which I blame on my childhood sweetheart, Max. I felt betrayed and hurt at the ripe old age of six, and never really got over it. I went through a phase in my late twenties when I went to therapy, read self-help books, attended yoga classes, and even took a trip to India, where I stayed in an ashram for two weeks to, according to the slick website, "evolve and grow spiritually." Although my attempts moved the needle a bit with self-discovery, I was still left with an emptiness that no one could fill. With all that investment in myself, you would think I would have figured it out, or at least come to understand the meaning of letting go. The memory and feelings haunt me, despite how much I try to release the demons of my boy-crush past.

Of course, Derrick is here before me. Annoying. Part of me appreciated that he was always so punctual, but another part of me always felt the pressure to be ready on time. He is so incredibly handsome—raw and masculine—such a guy's guy. Thank God, he is not one of those Manhattan metrosexuals who use more hair products than I do and get manicures! My finely crafted, aloof, and controlled exit plan quickly turns into sadness. What a waste of a man! He looks good on the outside, but is so damaged on the inside. He's like a shiny Red Delicious apple, but as you take a bite, you realize that it is rotten to the core. I thought this relationship had so much promise and possibility, and now it is over. I have to pick my heart up off the floor and exit gracefully. No pun intended. Well, maybe a little.

It is uncharacteristically quiet in Starbucks this evening. Usually, it is difficult to find a seat because students and entrepreneurs fill every table with their laptops and three-hour coffees, abandoned and cold, taking up space. It's six thirty, normally a busy time with a flurry of orders for people staying late in the office or connecting with friends after work. Personally, I always prefer happy hour with a quality glass of red wine or the occasional craft cocktail.

But tonight, I think meeting him with alcohol in my system is a bad idea. I know that I would either curse him out or go to bed with him one last time. Both options scream unhealthy, so thankfully I know and respect my limitations. I am not strong enough to do the right thing if alcohol is brought into the equation. Although alcohol would help numb the pain, even if it were short-lived.

I find him easily at a table towards the back. I am relieved that we won't be sitting on top of people; that would add to the humiliation of the moment. Derrick stands up as I approach him. He is good like that, very polite, brought up with good manners. He always held open the door, brought around the car when it was raining, and made sure I was on the inside of the street as we walked through the city. He was there to protect me from any cars or bikes that may swerve towards us. He would have been the one to take the hit, and for me, that was love. I have never understood why women scoff at a man who holds the door open, lets her go first through the door, or brings her flowers. I love that; it makes me feel taken care of, and I appreciate it. New Yorkers live in a concrete jungle, so who wouldn't appreciate a bouquet of nature in their apartment? As independent as I am, I never understood that.

Derrick speaks first, "Hi, Grace. Wow, you look great." He seems surprised as his voice skips an octave higher. "I got us a seat, and I'll get your drink. What do you want?"

I do not acknowledge the compliment. I do not want to give him anything; I am too upset. *Take a good look at what you are going to be missing, asshole.* But, of course, I just answer his question, playing it cool. Or at least put up a front that I am okay with all of this. "I'll take a tall decaf." That is the best option since my caffeine intake is at an all-time high. I am so wired that I feel like I'm jumping out of my skin.

Derrick makes his way to the counter to place the order as I sit down and put his duffle bag of stuff on the empty chair next to me. How sad it is that after three years, all the bag contains is a razor, deodorant, two pairs of Calvin Klein black boxer briefs, and a ratty

Giants sweatshirt. I hadn't wanted to give the sweatshirt back because I know he loves that rag. He wore it almost every time he got comfy on the couch, which was quite often. For him, that sweatshirt represents his childhood, the love of football, and his beloved NFL team. Being in the sweatshirt is home, no matter when or where he wears it. Returning it is the right thing to do, but I admit deep down I want Derrick to feel immense pain at this moment, and losing that sweatshirt would hit right at his heart. The bag had been packed, minus the sweatshirt, and sitting on my kitchen counter, ready to grab as I walked out the door for work this morning. In the end, I just could not do it. I went back to the bedroom, pulled the ratty shirt out of the otherwise-empty top drawer, and stuffed it in the bag.

He has brought me nothing, which is what I was expecting. I can count on one hand the number of times I spent the night at his apartment. At most, there might have been a pair of pj's, a change of underwear and socks, but that is all. I preferred being in my own space, and he always offered to come over. The fact that he did not even return those few items is telling. He probably has no clue that my stuff is still in the drawer. I really want his next girlfriend to find my underwear, although it is the everyday cotton stuff, not the Agent Provocateur variety. It gives me satisfaction thinking about how uncomfortable that conversation will be.

When Derrick returns with my coffee, I clutch it like a lifeline and look out the window. The city is filled with high-octane energy, people moving in every corner; it is frenetic out there. Occasionally, I contemplated living somewhere with a slower pace, but then I would get sucked into the allure of the bright lights and big city of Manhattan—dollar slices of pizza, ability to walk anywhere, parks, and knowing there is always something open, twenty-four hours a day. Some of the people passing by the window are laughing; most are walking briskly and talking on their cell phones, while others are being led by their miniature dogs, their babies. Even though I am surrounded by strangers everywhere, Manhattan has always been home since day one.

Derrick sits down and stares at me with blank eyes, his gaze empty, disconnected, and numb. I don't recognize him anymore. When we first dated, I would open the front door, and there he would be, his eyes sparkling with joy and an honest brightness of anticipation; he was excited to see me. I felt it even during that first five-second exchange. Tonight, there is no light in those eyes; they are just gray and very flat. There is no more "us," and we both know it.

Derrick, seeming almost relieved, actually smiles and blurts, "So this is it?" As if he were a short-order cook, and I just ordered the small fries. It would be an understatement to say that sometimes he lacked interpersonal sensitivity.

I usually let it go and don't let it impact me, but in this moment I feel differently. I say nothing. I am frozen, paralyzed neck up. I am doing everything to hold back and keep from losing my shit. The emotions rising up in me like an erupting volcano. When I get to that point, there is no coming back and usually no survivors when I finally boil over.

Derrick feels compelled to fill the silence. "Grace, I'm sorry that it didn't work out. Good luck." I know that was he is speaking the truth, and he cannot keep up the façade any longer.

In the beginning he seemed so capable, strong, the man I had been longing my entire life. But that has turned out to not be the case. He is a boy trapped in a man's body. Deep down, he wants no responsibility and does not want the same things out of life as I do. I cringe as the words come out of his mouth, but I feel it in my bones that is his truth. He is not capable of being in a partnership. He is looking to be saved, and I know I can't do that for him or anyone. Resentment would seep in the minute I made that deal.

I need to give myself the compassion and love that I desperately need in this moment. But how? During the relationship, it was all about Derrick and his feelings and emotions. I fell short when it came to owning my own emotional well-being. It is always easier to take care of others.

"Me too," I snap. "Here's your stuff. Goodbye, Derrick." There is no space for drawn-out goodbyes, reminiscing on the good times, or even room for one final hug. I look at him for the last time, snatch up my tall decaf, and command my legs to walk me out the door. *Just get out the door, and for God's sake, don't look back.* Why waste a perfectly good cup of coffee, especially on an ex?

I power walk for a couple of blocks, as if I have an appointment to keep, taking in deep breaths of air. I am not ready to go back to my empty apartment. My pace slows, and the tears start as I reflect on the past six months of our relationship. How could I have read it wrong? How could I not see his real motives? I work in marketing, for God's sake. It is my job to size people up, examine human behavior, and understand their real needs and wants. In the end, all Derrick's actions pointed to his looking for a free ride, for me to carry him and his baggage. I was the savior who rode in on the white horse, wearing a shiny coat of armor. By the last month, I had only disgust for Derrick, and simultaneously became enraged with myself. How many times did I ask myself, shaking my head in shame, *How could I have been such a fool?* I believed him when he said I was special enough that he would take that chance and get married again. We even looked at rings! His idea, not mine. I never even pushed the notion. He told me that he wanted to know what I liked so that he would choose wisely when the time came for him to make the big purchase. All part of his empty promises.

Adding to the "together forever" fantasy, we even started to look at apartments. Trying to find an affordable, quality home in Manhattan was no small feat. Once we realized that we couldn't afford the city, we ventured farther out to the other boroughs—Queens and Brooklyn. And that's when it really started to unravel for me. I saw his incompetence and discovered how clueless he was about taking that next step. As we started to work with a realtor, I found his approach to apartment hunting juvenile when it came to what we needed and what we could afford. He was all about the aesthetics—high-end appliances, rooftop decks, and a lobby that sparkled. I even asked him once, "Why do you care about those details? In the scheme of things, they are so trivial."

I have such a practical side, looking at the numbers, analyzing the statistics. Those are the traits that make me a success as a senior market research and insights manager. I am obsessed with data and all about quantitative and qualitative information. I am about looking at the numbers. "Let's create a spreadsheet to see if we can afford this apartment," I suggested. My approach was practical. The rooftop was usable for about five months of the year, if that. We traveled through the lobby twice a day for maybe two minutes in total. Our quality time would be spent lounging on the couch or cooking dinner together in the kitchen. The most important part of the whole apartment search was our commitment to live together in a true partnership, one in which we would have each other's backs, make coffee together in the morning, snuggle up together as we fell asleep.

In the end, I realized we were both going through the motions. His motivation was to get out of his shit box of an apartment and mine was fueling my delusions of living happily ever after with him. I guess the expression "Love is blind" came into play. Deep down, I did not want to admit the things I did not like about Derrick; he was a person who bounced from job to job, had $30K in credit-card debt, and professed hatred for the rich and capitalism. Money would be a struggle for the rest of our lives, and I would be forced to carry his dead weight.

There were signs, especially over the last six months. In the end, my sense of self was kicking and screaming. My intuition was trying desperately to get my attention. *Grace, please listen to me. Something is not right here.* My anxiety, sadness, and anger were at an all-time high. Instead, I ignored my instincts and was intoxicated by future possibilities. It was all about him; I was consumed with his drama, talking about all of his health problems, financial challenges, and work issues. The more I gave, the more he took. It was always some sob story, someone else's fault; he even blamed the government for his problems. Not once did he own his own shit or even man up. In the end, deep in my soul, I felt majorly betrayed, and that is what hit me the hardest. He wasted my time. He was never going to come through.

The reality was I had betrayed myself by believing in the delusion. Deep down, that was the toughest part of the situation to admit and make peace with. I put more weight on his empty words than on my feelings of anxiety and fear every time he came from a place of victimhood, shared his woes, and dumped his problems on me. I should have known better. I am not some naïve twenty-year-old. I am in my forties, and this was not my first relationship.

I was exhausted and disgusted that I invested so much time in something that turned out to be a very toxic dead end. And had nothing to show for it. I was back to square one and have to say it was very humbling.

His assurances and declarations along the way all meant squat. No follow-through and no action. His low emotional intelligence (EQ) astonished me. He is not emotionally capable of comprehending how hurtful and painful his hollow words are. He really doesn't care, and he never will. He is a textbook narcissist, one who can manipulate and get what he wants. If he doesn't get his way, then he is racing to the door to find the next naïve person. In the last weeks, he would repeat, "I can't make you happy. Maybe someone else is out there for you. I am tired of trying. Maybe this just won't work."

He was checked out and spent a lot of time on his phone, right in front of me. One time, I thought he was on a dating app, but he quickly got off before I could be entirely sure. He was more concerned about moving on and finding the love that he felt he deserved. The body of our relationship was not even cold yet, and he already was thinking about replacing me.

My insecurity bubbled up, and I questioned, *Why was I not enough? Did I not matter?* It was the worst feeling to realize I was nothing more than a minor detail in his life, just a blip on the radar. No one wants to be replaced easily, especially as they are breaking up. One core human value is about people feeling that they matter, especially to the ones whom they love.

And that is the real issue. He has no depth, is completely disconnected from his own heart and his ability to feel. In the end, I realized that I would never be emotionally safe with him and could never trust him enough to be vulnerable with him. Game over.

It is not only about the pain of my loss; it is the shame of it all. Because I'd dated before and failed. It took me a solid year to really let him in, both literally and figuratively. I gave him a key to my apartment, he was front and center on my Facebook page, and I even took him to major events, whether it be a work-award trip, Christmas with my family, or even my college reunion. In my forty-two years, I can count the number of boyfriends on one hand whom I introduced to my family.

Trusting men and believing relationships will work out has never been my strong suit. Deep down, I truly felt it wouldn't last, and I would have to rationalize to my friends and family why again my relationship did not work out. Shame is a tough pill for me to swallow. I pride myself on my strength and independence. Nothing stops me. Even as a child, I would say, "I can do it." Something within me takes real satisfaction in being able to handle any task on my own.

One therapist told me, "Your strong sense of self-reliance could be a blessing or maybe at times a curse." I am not going to be a damsel in distress so that the man can feel strong. No way. Men always comment that I am hard to read and come across very closed. I guess, if I take the time to reflect, there may be some truth to what they were saying. I loathe asking for help and showing any vulnerability. Receiving from others is a tough feat, and trust is not something I give out daily, especially when it comes to men.

All men have a pattern. In the beginning, they are on their best behavior, bring me flowers, take me out to nice restaurants, and hold open the car door. Time goes by and something shifts; they suddenly become stingy with their time, money, and presence. Their generosity fades away, along with any kind of effort to make me happy. I never understood why that change happened; all I know is, when it did, things went downhill fast from that point. It was a bait and switch.

This new reality of being alone once again is salt in my wound of unworthiness. Now, more than ever, I question whether someone could really love me and accept my entire self, especially when it comes to my flaws.

Back when Derrick asked me to look at rings, I would imagine that it was right before New Year's when I would be showing off my engagement ring that sparkled, while my man hugged me real tight as we both announced with joy the big news. Not this guy, not this year. Who knows, maybe with no one…ever. Maybe that was my ending.

The wind is picking up, and it is beginning to rain. The cold, sharp kind of drops. Isn't this just perfect? It is not bad enough wasting two years of my life by dating a narcissist who promised the world and could not deliver on his promises. Now I am going to lose a quality blowout with this weather, and I will be completely soaked by the time I get home. *What a fucking day! Dammit. Here come the tears.* If I pick up the pace, I can catch the light and cross at Greenwich. I feel the phone buzzing in my pocket, and I would like to be strong enough not to look, but I just have to know if it is Derrick. So what if I cannot answer.

There are some empty tables outside the cafes, so I sit down to finish my drink under my umbrella. As the skies open up, I stand, walk away, wipe my tears, take a deep breath, and start to cross the street. I always relish the freedom to cross the street when no cars are coming, religiously disregarding the traffic signs. Jaywalking was my finest act of rebellion, not that anyone even paid attention. The visibility was bleak as the skies opened. My next thought was interrupted as my phone buzzed; there was an iMessage.

Being in this emotional fog made me completely distracted and unaware of my surroundings. I was not paying attention to the taxicabs and Ubers fighting for real estate on the streets. And the minute

I took my eyes off the road and glanced at the iMessage, I saw bright lights and heard loud screeching noises. Time stood still. Everything and everyone blanked out. In that moment, my life changed forever. Nothing would ever be the same; the breakup was the least of my problems.

♡

Exploration Questions
Chapter 1

Grace

1. When do you know it is time to end a relationship? Do you initiate it or does your partner?

2. If you had the opportunity for a breakup do-over, what would you say or do differently?

3. If you could see one ex again, who would it be, and what would you need to say to, or hear from, them for closure?

4. Have you ever stayed too long in a relationship? If so, what prevented you from getting out earlier?

5. How do you listen to your gut when you are in a relationship?

Chapter 1 Activity

Foster Self-Care: List 5 ways you plan to nurture yourself in the next 30 days. This is especially important when you are going through a tough time in your life (e.g., losses, breakups, big changes). Self-care = Self-love.

Chapter 2

Lorenzo (Enzo)

Here I am, wobbling along Little West Street. Clearly, I am not wearing the right shoes. My heels are getting stuck, and I'm losing my balance on this cobblestone street. They're pretty, but not practical, especially with all the walking we do here in Manhattan.

And here's Pastis, one of my favorites. I am so sad right now. He ruined this too. Derrick first introduced me to this restaurant on our one-year anniversary. He knew how much I obsessed over Paris; the chic atmosphere featured French bistro fare, which delights my taste buds. Maybe it was the French onion soup *gratinée*, the *moules-frites*, or beef *bourguignon*. Out of the three, the beef bourguignon is the dish that connects with my soul. No contest.

Hang on, where are all these people going? What are they looking at? I can't see through the sea of black umbrellas. Umbrellas are a nuisance and an unnecessary evil, always getting in my way when I'm trying to get from point A to B. Annoying!

There's a crowd now standing around, I think, a woman lying in the street. Curiosity gets the best of me, and I push my way in to look too. Okay, that's a creepy coincidence; she is wearing the same dress as I am. I can say she has some kick-ass style. And here I am, feeling sorry for myself, when clearly her day has been much worse. God, she even looks like me. A lot like me. Wait. What?

Oh my God. Oh shit, am I dead? Is that *my* lifeless body lying there with all these strangers just staring at me? Are you kidding me? I die after a breakup, with a fabulous dress on? And now look at my blowout. My hair is ruined, full of dirt, black gravel, and rainwater. How can I be here and there at the same time? What happened? Maybe I'll wake up. That's it. Maybe I can jump back in my body or something, like in the movies. When the ambulance comes, everything will be okay.

Wait a minute, something or someone is coming towards me, the me on the ground. A tall man in a white robe with an Italian flag on the sleeve. He is surrounded by a golden-white aura, and he is smiling at me. Not sure what's happening here, although I am feeling quite a bit lighter. It's as though I am floating in clouds, both literally and figuratively. Am I in a movie here? This man leaning in toward me could be a character in *The Godfather* or *Goodfellas*. He reminds me of the character of Henry Hill played by Ray Liotta. I love that scene where he kicks the shit out of the guy who was harassing his girlfriend. I love that kind of passion. I wish a man had done that for me at least once in my life.

The man turns from the woman on the ground—me?—and walks over to where I am standing and watching this unreal scene unfold. "Grace, you know you are dead, but there's no need to worry about that. I am here to help."

Who is this paesano, and what the hell is he doing here? And what does he mean when he says not to worry about it?

The man laughs because he finds my reaction slightly amusing, and in a raspy voice he says, "Wow, Grace, you took quite a fall… on your ass!" He extended his hand and introduced himself, "I am Lorenzo; call me Enzo. And yeah, I may look like an angel, but, trust me, during my days on Earth, I was the furthest thing from an angel. But I made a deal with God when I was on Earth. He helped me out when I was in a bad situation, so I owed him. And now I am in the role, helping humanity. Go figure. The job has surprised me. I help souls find their way and complete what they were set out here on Earth to do. I am kind of like the 'purpose whisperer.'" Then he busts out a big, hearty laugh.

"You're probably thinking, 'What the hell am I doing here, right? I am your guide, and I am here to help. I chose you. And, trust me, I don't just pick people on a whim. I need to know that we'll connect and be on the same page. Otherwise, it's a struggle, and people can be a pain in the ass. You already know that. There's a lot happening in this moment. How are you doing? This is quite a change, and I am throwing lots of info at you. It is a lot to take in. Are you okay?'"

Normally, I'm leery when strange men approach me, but for some reason this guy feels safe. And I can relate to what he's saying. People can bring a lot of drama to certain situations. I find it exhausting. I want answers, and maybe this guy—or this spirit, or whatever he is—can give them to me. Plus, he picked me. Picked me for what? This intrigues me. I always liked being selected first when it came to being chosen for soccer.

I am so confused, and the anxiety is starting to creep. My life is over? I don't understand. I am too young to die. There's so much I was supposed to accomplish. What is this guy doing here? He says he is here to help. What is he, an angel or something? I am regretting that I did not attend church as much as I probably should have. I'm not an atheist, but I always yearned for a stronger spiritual connection with God. I did not make the time, and now my guilt is kicking in. Am I even supposed to be feeling this?

If I am dead, where's the white light? I am having trouble paying attention to what he is saying. I am trying to understand how this could happen to me. Even with the sirens screaming and lights approaching, I am still in denial. Luckily, Enzo's presence blocks the scene from my view. It is just too weird to see myself that way. Still trying to ground myself and figure out what just happened, I look at him and ask, "What now?"

I have to trust him at this moment. I don't want to, but what choice do I have? No one else can see me. The me that is standing here. All the others are focused on a lifeless body, wondering who she is and how she ended up here?

Enzo startles me. "Hey, let's get out of here. Let's change it up. Too many people here. I hate a crowd."

Enzo places his hand over his heart, and then we travel someplace else. It happens so fast that I am thrown off. How does he do this? I like this magical way of traveling. Will I get that superpower?

Interestingly enough, we arrive at my favorite place. The sun is out, the trees are in bloom, and it is peaceful. There are a few people running around Central Park's Reservoir. I love this place. I would come here at 6:00 a.m. to think and run. It was so calming for me. My days always went smoother when I went for a run. Getting out of bed was not so easy, but when I did, I would always treat myself to an Americano at Bluestone Lane Café. I am starting to come to terms that I may never be able to run again in the flesh. Maybe that is why I am here. To say goodbye to the park, my happy place. I guess it is really starting to sink in that I am dead.

"Grace, I know this is your happy place."

Holy crap, can he read my mind?

"That's why we are here, to give you a sense of familiarity since everything else around you is changing rapidly."

"Why are you here? Are you, like, my guardian angel or something?"

"I am a helper. You might say I am a guide, a spirit guide for souls who have crossed over. I work with the big guy upstairs and help people resolve some stuff that remains from their life on Earth. I relay God's messages and help bring your soul's path to a meaningful completion. You're going to be taking it to a new level. Because your life was cut short, there are understandings that you will never get to experience. Unfortunately, you did not learn all the lessons. So now you have to course correct, do it now in a new way. That's why I am here. To bail you out."

"Next level? I am not even good enough dead?"

"Wait a minute here, Grace. This is not a good road to go down. It's kind of like graduating from high school, not that I ever experienced that. School and I did not get along. Never finished. Dropped out. You get an opportunity to experience a higher level of education, more like college. Of course, no pomp and circumstance, or the cap and gown. Those traditions are quite trivial in the afterlife."

"So God is giving me an opportunity? What about others? Do they have to do this? I am not sold."

"Not gonna lie. No, this is not for everyone. As guides, we help people who are willing to put in the work. No dead weight. Otherwise, what a waste of energy. I chose you because you are direct and don't put up with people's shit. And at the same time, there is a softness about you. When it comes to relationships you have been through a lot. You remind me of me in certain aspects. You love coffee and food. Two things I was passionate about when I was alive. Plus, we met once before, in a past life. All I can say for now is that I owe you. I saw your name on my list of souls to work with, and I knew you were no slacker, so I chose you. You are a straight shooter; our personalities are probably going to be in sync. Not like oil and water. You have a tough exterior, yet your heart is good. I got in much more trouble than you, but still, at the core, we are similar. My job is to support your soul's journey.

"Prior to birth, as souls we take on special assignments. We even sign an official contract that details what we plan to learn in our next lifetime. Unfortunately, your journey was cut short. Not to worry, Grace, I'm here to save the day. Let's face it; you'll do all the heavy lifting here. But I will make sure you are heading in the right direction, so you can understand your true purpose. This way you can move forward after you finish what you started here."

Maybe I am in a fog because of the accident. After all, that woman in the street, me, seems to have a pretty serious head injury. Or maybe I am in denial. "Cut short?! I don't get it. How do you even know me? Or should I say you're my soul guide? My head is spinning. I just want to go back to the time when I was getting the blowout, or even when I was heading to Starbucks. I wish—"

"Well, let me put it to you this way. As you were crossing the street and checking your IM, you didn't see that Tesla coming straight at you. This is where destiny and free will intersect. The driver swerved, but still hit you, and you went over like rag doll. Physically, you couldn't recover, and now they are taking away your body. Game over. No more physical Grace living in NYC."

"Isn't there supposed to be a white light or a tunnel, or something peaceful? Now you are telling me I have more work to do because I got hit by a car. Are you kidding me?" Now I am getting aggravated.

"Yep, you still have work to do. Yeah, kinda sucks, but you have me to help. This is not my first rodeo, as I have helped many. This lifetime is over now, but your soul's contract is incomplete. On Earth, we are given the power of free will. How you live your life is up to each person. Our soul has a contract, and at the end of our time on Earth, we hope we've delivered on our promises and do right on our contract. Sometimes, people fall a bit short, while others have an epic fail. For you, it is a tad short, but the good news is that you have been given a bit more time to carry out what you were meant to do in this lifetime. It is not a punishment, but a privilege. You get to work with me."

Enzo smiles as he tries to make a joke. I am not in the mood. I did just die, for God's sake. I don't know; maybe I was supposed to feel sad, but instead, I headed straight for my go-to emotion, which is anger. Deep down, rage is my favorite emotion. I love the intensity of the plethora of energy that goes with it. It would usually end with a major release of tears, but it still gave me some strength even if it was short-lived and brief. Now I feel cheated and majorly pissed off.

I knew that phone would be the death of me. I was always checking in, day and night. And where did that get me?! My last day on Earth, and I was breaking up with a loser guy. Are you kidding me?! Well, at least I had a nice dress on and was sporting a fabulous blow-out. Of course, that stain will never come out.

"Did you hear me? Grace, Grace…"

Hearing my name brought me back to the present moment. "Yes, I did. Oh my God, you are telling me that I am dead?! I can't believe this. What do I do now? Oh crap, what the hell is next?" *Oh my God, wait a minute. I probably shouldn't be saying those words. I don't want to piss off anyone here.*

Enzo took control of the conversation, or should I say took the wheel as I was veering into a ditch. "Okay, this is no time to freak out. Snap out of it! Let's keep focused."

Is he quoting *Moonstruck?* I hate when people tell me to relax when I am freaking out.

He softens his tone and changes it up because he's probably getting the sense that he's just making my blood boil now. "Grace, that is what I am here for; you are not alone. I am here to guide you and help you get to the next level and learn the lessons. Although I have strict orders not to do the work for you. I am a sounding board and will make sure you are on the right path. Ultimately, it is your journey, and you have to do the work and heavy lifting. I am here for moral support and to let you know when you are fucking up. Crap, I was told I needed to work on my language. Well, you know what I mean."

I appreciate his rawness and think it is funny that he gets scolded from up above on his language. I love to curse, although I tempered it around clients, not so much in front of my colleagues. Maybe we are a good match; we can work on that cussing thing together.

"I think I am going to need another Americano for this journey. Can you help me out with that?"

He could hardly get the words out for laughing. "Do I look like a barista?"

I guess that's a no. Great, the first thing I ask him to do, and he is already falling short. What kind of guardian angel is he anyway? Don't they have a magic wand or special talents from the divine? The strange part is, I like his edge. It makes me feel incredibly safe with him. He is real and tells it like it is. No sugarcoating it. I need the support right now. He will keep me on track and do it in a direct manner. Quite frankly, that is probably more important for the journey than a coffee, although I am already missing sitting at the Bluestone, a strong, warm cup of Americano goodness nestled between my hands. I'm going to miss coffee. And my barista.

I love my barista; he knows my name and order by heart. I wonder if he will miss me. Or notice I'm not coming in anymore. He always appreciated my designer dresses and commented on them; he attended Fashion Week every year, so he was knowledgeable.

I was used to a level of service, especially living in Manhattan. It came at a price, but I didn't care. Maybe I should have been a bit *more* extravagant. The last apartment I looked at had a balcony and a view of Central Park. That extra $500 a month would have provided me the space to enjoy my glass of wine while looking out at the greenery of Manhattan. And I should have said yes to the long weekend in Nice. That 401K money was a waste, although it will go to my parents now. That should help pay back the college tuition they gave me.

I am still coming to terms with this new adventure. It doesn't look as if there is any way to get out of this or to escape this self-discovery. There is a part of me that does not trust Enzo. Let's face it; I did not trust many here on Earth, especially men. He needs to earn it. I don't know him. Well, at least in this lifetime. This whole situation is bizarre, and I am trying to wrap my head around it. Humbly, I ask, "Okay, where should I start?"

I could tell Enzo was trying to be kind, but he was rough around the edges. He couldn't help it. "I find that some are good with intimate relationships. Others, not so much. Grace, my dear, that is you—not so good at relationships. Whether we like it or not, our insecurities come out, and we make a mess out of things. Relationships challenge us to grow. It's not only about the other person, but an opportunity for our souls to expand and grow. It is part of your soul's contract. Your life was cut short by being on that damn phone. So you are getting one more shot to finish what you started."

"Can I jump back into my body, get one more opportunity?"

Enzo replied, "No, Grace. This is not how it works. That time has passed. You need to look forward. I will help you do that. You do have to trust me, and I feel you don't yet. So that is your first task—be vulnerable enough to trust me. You see me as a stranger although I am not. I knew you before, but you have forgotten. I'll get into that later. For now, you have to have a little faith here. I am a straight shooter, so no BS from me. That I can promise you."

I was the type of person who needed to see it before I believed it. I knew that mindset wouldn't work here. Nothing made sense; although when Enzo spoke, I listened. I mean, at this point, what other choice did I have? I had to walk forward into the unknown, no certainty. The only thing I did know was that I was terrified. What if I did not get the lesson or complete the task or tasks? If I didn't complete it when I was alive, how can I do it now?

I could be a very black-and-white person, especially as I got older. Self-help books, shows like Oprah's *Super Soul Sunday*, or even the Hay House channel, were not really my thing, except for that brief phase of exploration in my early twenties. My friends who were coaches would say things to me, like, "Every day you breathe you are mani-festing your life. Only you have the power to change what is on the inside, and that will transform the outside." I felt it was woo-woo stuff. They always meant well, but deep down I felt that they were referring to everyone else; what they said didn't apply to me.

It made me feel completely ill-equipped because what was happen-ing on the outside was not even close to what I imagined my life would be. I didn't always like what was coming my way, whether it was the men, the bosses, or even the friends I hung out with. They all looked good at first, but when I really got to see their "bones," it was not so good. Some relationships bothered me more, hit home, but with others, I just said, "It's their shit, not mine." Maybe that was a deflection. I am definitely not a psychologist here.

Enzo started to drill down with a few more specifics. "The first thing you are going to do is connect back with the men you dated. Not to worry. Not *every* man, that would take a century."

His joke even made me smile.

"You'll be visiting guys who you have encountered throughout your life. Men or boys that had pivotal roles in your life. They shaped how you saw the male species and even how you viewed yourself in relationships."

"Hold on, Enzo. What do you mean, I'll be visiting these guys? Am I going to be haunting people?"

"Okay, I need to explain that better. You see, on this side, time is different. We don't experience things in a linear way, not like on Earth when one thing happens before another. You will be moving through time, reliving things from you past, and then experiencing the future. Luckily, it will happen in a flash, so it is not the travel you're used to."

I say, "Not sure what all of this means. But I guess I have to go with it."

Enzo continues, not really acknowledging my response, "There is a specific reason why each one was handpicked, or shall I say 'heart picked,' from up above. This exercise is all about growth and extracting the meaning from each experience. Get ready, Grace. As you embark on this journey, you'll be discovering deeper connections within yourself and what you were meant to learn. It is not about getting it right; it is about exploring parts of yourself you were scared to experience in the moment.

"It is not only about you; we all reside in the same universe, which is multidimensional and complex, and at the end of the day, you'll know we are all connected. Here on Earth, you humans speak about individualization, being independent and out on your own. When you speak with others, you approach life as 'What's yours is yours, and what's mine is mine.' And yes, it is true that there is one spirit to one body, but we are far more connected than separated.

"Taking this notion into action, your assignment is to help those people that are in your path. Like you, they too have to own their part in the relationship while you are having your own personal revelation. It takes two to tango. You'll know when you are finished with each task. The end goal here is to complete your journey of love and your soul contract. Forgive, let go, and love. Let's get down to the practical nature of the assignment."

"Okay, that's something I can get on board with. Now we're talking."

Enzo smirked. "There's not much practicality and concreteness about this task, which will frustrate you. You want to see the facts, the data, and a manual to figure out this quest. There is no instruction guide. The learning is on an energetic and spiritual level. The time travel will be led by me. I have that power. I will be sure to get you to each destination. The tools and skills will come from you. Just know you can't think your way out of it; you won't find it in your head. You will be using your feelings and intuition to uncover the messages. You will find yourself in the past, present, and future. You will quickly know which dimension you are in once you see everyone involved.

"Although it may seem that you are alone, that's not the case. I am here. That's my job. I won't be giving you the answers, though. Think of me as your partner in crime in your adventure. Trust yourself; listen to keep on track. In the physical life, you were in your head; now, you're going to be using your heart and guts. The question isn't 'What do you think?' The question is 'How do you feel?'"

Suddenly, I feel like I am already connected to my intuition. It is a bit foreign. It is already speaking with me as I feel a heaviness in my stomach, like a lump of coal within my center. *Oh God, how am I going to handle this? I couldn't handle relationships when I was alive, let alone now. Haven't I had enough lessons? When does it end?*

My anger ebbed, and in flowed the sadness. Finding true love had been such a struggle for me, and I really did try. Speaking with Enzo brought my defensive nature to light. "Why am I getting punished here? Isn't it bad enough that my life was cut short as the consequence of my behavior—being on the phone while crossing the street? That was indeed a bad habit, although it's a habit common to many New Yorkers as they travel the streets. Can't I graduate like other people do when they die? Why must this limbo be prolonged for me? Was I that terrible of a person?"

"Grace, this is not a punishment; it is an opportunity," he said seriously. "My Father has great faith in you and wanted to give your soul the chance to make it to that next level. We don't usually give these opportunities to people. Usually, they have to replay their story again in another body, with new circumstances, and sometimes even with heightened challenges. Basically, they live it over and over until they complete the learning, their soul contract. It can take centuries to get it right. Although time is more of a human construct, we feel it as limitless.

"That's another reason I picked you. I owe you, and you will understand as you go through the journey. For now, I've told you what you need to know at this point. You are a quick study. Again, it just got cut short, but with the last breakup, you were in the midst of a huge transformation. My hope is that you can see this as a blessing, that you have the support and love throughout the experience to graduate to the next level."

How the hell am I going to do this? I couldn't figure this out in the real world. Now I have to go back and try it again? Dating and relationships were painful to experience the first time. And this time, I have to endure it without my trusty Jack and Coke to take the edge off. *Second chance? It sounds more like hell.* On the bright side, I won't have to worry about the hangovers. Not going to need Advil, saltine crackers, and Gatorade to get me through. Looking back, maybe my packed schedule, the drinking, and the hangovers were just ways of avoiding the sadness that was waiting for me inside of every unguarded moment.

"No. No. Can't do it." Even I could hear the panic rising in my voice.

Enzo picked up on it, of course. "Grace, it's about having faith in the process, in me...and more importantly, in yourself. I wouldn't put you into a situation that you couldn't handle. Step into the unknown, and trust that all will resolve itself. I'm not saying that it won't be challenging, but I am saying you have all the love within you to heal what comes your way. Also, you can always call out to me, and I will support you. Let's not delay. What are your questions?"

I put my big girl panties on and stepped into unfamiliar territory. "When do we get started?" It was my opportunity to complete what I started in the flesh forty-two years ago as Grace Isabella Anderson. I tapped into any semblance of bravery that I had in the depth of my soul to embrace what was ahead of me.

♡

Exploration Questions
Chapter 2
Lorenzo (Enzo)

1. Is there a particular moment that changed the trajectory of your life?

2. What would you want your spirit guide to be like? Would he be a tough guy like Enzo? Or would she be a glowing angel with a soft voice and gently flapping wings?

3. How would you want your spirit guide to help you?

4. Which former relationship would you absolutely NOT want to revisit and why?

5. Grace really loves her coffee. Which food or drink would you miss most in the afterlife?

Chapter 2 Activity

Create a Spiritual-Abundance Collage: Put on uplifting music, and choose pictures that represent how spirituality is present in your life and how it can grow. Spirituality is different for everyone. It could be asking God for help, statements of gratitude, meditation, joining a Bible-study group, connecting with your intuition, or walking in nature. Be creative and have fun!

Chapter 3

Max and Jesse

*W*ait *a minute. Where am I?* I am in a different time and place. That was quick. Enzo made it happen in a blink of an eye. So this place is familiar, yet I feel uncomfortable, very unsettled. It is like I have been here before. I find myself in front of a small brick-front home with a white screen door. I am standing on the walkway, right next to a maple tree. The sun is going in and out behind the clouds. I smell the green grass, and I am surrounded by similarly sized homes. There's not a lot of traffic; one or two cars have gone by, and I saw a teenage boy speed by on his black ten-speed Schwinn. It makes me think of my yellow bike with the white front basket covered with daisies. I loved riding around the neighborhood. And let me not forget the bell attached to the handlebars; I put a sparkly red heart decal on it. I rang that bell every time I rode up the driveway. *Ding, ding, ding, ding…* I miss that sound.

What am I doing here? Why am I back here? What should I be doing? I am already discouraged, and I'm not even a minute into the process. Or whatever you call it—journey, transformation…who knows. I have my first assignment, and I am completely lost. This is going to be a long voyage. *Where's my caffeine to guide me through this?*

My past began to replay an important event, one that I had forgotten for a long time, until it crept into my consciousness. Repressed memories resurfaced in my twenties—damn that yoga meditation retreat I went to in Tulum. Although I loved Tulum for its Caribbean simplicity, deep-blue water, and laid-back vibe, the sixty-minute meditation sessions were hell. And each day of the retreat we had to attend one morning, one afternoon, and one evening meditation. Trying to sit still and be with myself was torture. The sessions brought up a lot of crap that I could not bury back inside.

My best friend paid for this "self-development adventure" that she was sure would cure both of us of all our issues and heal us of our struggles. Hope was generous like that; even if she only had two nickels to rub together, she would go for the purchase anyway. She would put it on her credit card and worry about it at the end of the month. We were different in that way; the minute I spent the money, I was paying it off. I was taught to be responsible with money and to be debt-free. To carry a credit card balance would be a sacrilege.

For me, the trip was hell. It created a lot of turmoil and chaos, which resulted in two sessions a week with my therapist. At the time, I could not handle riches of emotional upheaval and wondered how I could get it back in the treasure chest, lock it, and throw away the key—guaranteed never to be opened again.

Focusing again on the scene before me, I notice the cute seven-year-old with a ponytail. The bow in her hair matches the rainbow-decal T-shirt and coordinating pink skirt she is wearing. *Wait a minute; I loved that shirt. Oh, I remember those sneakers.* As a kid, I was all about the sneakers. No fancy shoes for me until I hit seventeen years old.

As early as I can remember, I embraced my competitive side. I loved playing kickball. I must say I was very sporty and good at it. Yet I had a softer, nurturing side to me as well. All my baby dolls were well taken care of and loved.

As I look at the little girl's face, she seems all too familiar. Full of zest and sass, yet with an overwhelming need to be liked. The sacredness of her innocence is so beautiful and precious to see. I just want to kneel down and give her a big hug. *Hi, Little Grace, Big Grace is here.* I wanted her to know I am here for her.

Enzo appears in the blink of an eye and stands between Little Grace and me. Wow, that guy has superpowers; he pops in and out. He's good at the teleporting stuff. "She can't see you. She's not supposed to see you. This scene was the beginning of your insecurity and marks the moment when your issues with boys and men all started. It was not only about them, but it was also about you, your sense of self. There was a part of you that you lost and never seemed to recover."

Poof! He's gone! Vanished into thin air.

Suddenly, the pit in my stomach grows. A cloud of dread surrounds me. I know what is about to transpire, and I am not sure I can do anything about it. At the time, I could do nothing to save her—me, I should be saying. It was the inner child, Little Grace, whom I am uncovering; she stayed with me even as an adult. This can't be about my watching the scene play out again. What's the learning in that? I dreaded the thought that I may be paralyzed once again. The worst part was I already knew how this day was going to end before it even started.

I was a cute kid. Little Grace bounces to the door and opens it with a smile from ear to ear as she sees her next-door neighbor Max. From the moment I moved in, I always loved to be around Max. He was so adorable, and I was always drawn to something about him. He was my first friend. We would play outside a lot, riding our bikes around the cul-de-sac. I had strict orders to stay by the house, not roam too far from home base. Sometimes, we would wander into the woods, which came right up to my backyard, where there was a small stream that we could cross by hopping from rock to rock. Luckily, it was fairly shallow, so there was no real danger of sinking and drowning. On most days, we played hopscotch on my driveway. My favorite part was drawing the pattern with thick pieces of colored chalk.

Since Max was a few years older, I admired and trusted him. He was my boy crush. I wouldn't dare ever admit it to anyone. It was all very innocent. When he asked me to play outside, I would yell across the house, "Mom, going outside." And I would be out the door in a flash. It was almost like time would stop; hours would go by, and

I would lose myself. I was a strong, opinionated girl who said yes when she wanted something and no when she did not.

Around Max, I would become another version of myself. It was all about pleasing him and being agreeable. I lost a little of my sass and became a bit more bashful. Maybe because I liked him. I was drawn to tough little Max with the sweet smile. He could bring on the charm. It would be in full effect when his mom was angry with him.

He came from a working-class family. His parents worked a lot to support him and his two sisters. At times, they struggled to make ends meet. They wanted a good life for their children, a better one than what they had. Max was the oldest, but one time he told me that secretly he wished that he were the youngest. There was a part of him that was scared of his dad. His dad was quite hard on him, always telling him to take out the trash, help with the yard work, and babysit his younger siblings when his parents weren't home. To some degree, Max resented the extra responsibility because he wanted to be riding bikes with the cool crowd, the older boys.

There was a part of Max that enjoyed being around me. He knew that I liked him, and his ego reveled in that fact. I was very agreeable, maybe too much so. And I was spunky, and some boys found me quite cute and were drawn to my beautiful blue eyes. Even if Max liked me, he would never admit that out loud. He was taught from other boys in the neighborhood that being around girls wasn't the popular thing to do. The cooler thing was to see what kind of mischief they could get into without getting caught.

He loved football; he was a big Dallas Cowboys fan. I always found that kind of odd since he lived in the Tri-State area, where most people were loyal to their beloved New York Giants, although the Jets would be their first pick. It was hard not to be influenced based on the place you lived. These teams' hats, jerseys, and sweatshirts were at every sporting goods or department store within a sixty-mile radius.

But that is what I liked about him. He did what he wanted and did not care what others thought. I was drawn to that. But there were only a few things in his life Max felt that way about. I saw him get teased for his team of choice. I loved his conviction. His loyalty to his beloved team outweighed a little irritation from his classmates. He could not be persuaded to change his mind. His strong will would kick in. Although when it came to being liked or looking cool in front of his friends, Max would fold like a cheap suit. Unfortunately, I experienced this firsthand.

Today was a different scenario; Max brought another boy into the mix. Something about this boy was never right. I came to realize that Jesse was manipulative and had an agenda. He was twelve years old and lived three houses down from me. These days, we would describe Jesse's homelife as dysfunctional. His parents had just gotten divorced, and he was terribly angry about how broken his family was. His dad basically abandoned him after the divorce and didn't come around much, especially after he found a new girlfriend. He would stop by for a quick slice of pizza or would show up for the last few minutes of Jesse's soccer game.

But that was last fall, and now we were into summer. Jesse blamed everyone else for all the bad in his life, but it was his father that he was really angry with. Looking back, I understand the source of the rage in his eyes. Deep down, he wanted people to suffer for his pain and unhappiness. But I couldn't see it then; I was just a kid. Everyone around Jesse paid the price for his rage and pain. Casualties everywhere.

Since his mom worked, and there was little supervision after school, he usually hung out with the older crowd. In the woods, they had taken over an abandoned shed that they called "the fort." They filled it with old furniture they found on the street and hid their beer there. Jesse hated the taste of beer, and it made him feel sick, but he would accept the offer every time a bottle was passed around.

Jesse had been spending time with Max, who was younger, more innocent, and could be manipulated. They rode the bus together, and Max always followed Jesse's lead. Jesse liked the high of having the power and being the ringleader. He was the one in charge.

I watch Little Grace come out and see Jesse standing next to Max. At that time, I didn't know him; we went to different schools and were on different schedules. What I did know was that he lived down the street and that he and Max were friends.

Jesse took the lead in the conversation. "Hi, Grace, we're going to go to the playground. There are others there. Why don't you join us?"

Now it is all coming back to me. This scenario makes me so uneasy. I am going to see it play out again. I'll relive it. Little Grace pondered the idea, and I can see she is a bit hesitant. I knew the playground was a bit farther from home, and my parents always warned me to stay close and not go too far. But I… Well, Little Grace, would always jump at an opportunity to have fun, especially if Max was involved. And then I hear it; Little Grace says, "Okay, I'll play."

Jesse said, "Let's go."

I know that wheels are in motion, and there is nothing I can do. At the time, I was so innocent and bubbly. All I wanted was to have fun and play.

Little Grace begins twirling around as she skips to the playground. She embraces her feminine energy and enjoys wearing her dresses. I did love that time when I was more carefree. There was more peace within me.

I don't want Little Grace to go. *Please don't go! It is a trap. Where are Mom and Dad? Maybe they can stop this. Where are they so they can say that the playground is too far from home?* I feel so paralyzed as I watch from my afterlife sideline; there's nothing I can do. I feel helpless.

Little Grace is walking by herself and having a grand time, while Max and Jesse are talking. She has no clue; she's just skipping around in her pink miniskirt. I follow her. I can't leave her, even if she can't see me, because I know what is about to happen.

We've arrived. Wow, now being here, everything looks so much smaller. The playground only consists of a few items. It has a set of four swings, a sandbox with a random bucket and shovel that was left, a seesaw, a slide, and then the monkey bars. I remember it being larger and having lots of stuff to play on. Nowadays, playgrounds are much more elaborate.

Jesse starts talking to a group of five boys, just hanging out and laughing with one another. They are more his age and seem familiar to him. At the time, I was clueless and did not know who they were. I was always about playing with different people, so I didn't care.

Within five minutes of arriving at the playground, Jesse makes an announcement, "Hey, everyone, let's have a contest. Let's see who can cross the monkey bars the quickest. I can time everyone with my watch." He holds up the digital Casio watch that he got for his last birthday. He told Max it was the only present he liked. He never got anything, but he knew his parents felt a bit guilty about the divorce. He figured they should give him something; the divorce kind of ruined his life. Then Jesse says, "Girls first, Grace. You go first."

Little Grace looks around and realizes that she is the only girl. For some reason, she gets a little nervous. I can now see it in her eyes as she looks around and comes to that realization. But then she snaps out of it because she likes a fun game with some healthy competition. She played games with her siblings and cousins all the time. Super fun! Little Grace says with pride, "Okay, I'll go."

I know what happens next, and I am so uncomfortable. I want to stop the entire scene and hold Max down so he doesn't do what he is about to do. I don't have any power, just as I didn't in that moment as a seven-year-old. We are one and the same. That is true. I am Little Grace; she is my younger self.

As Little Grace is walking towards the monkey bars, Jesse starts chanting, "Grace, Grace, Grace," and then all the boys join in and continue saying her name.

I see Little Grace, and she is smiling and feeling good. All eyes are on her, and everyone seems to be smiling. In her mind, I know what she is thinking—*I got this; I can play with the big boys.*

In the meantime, as Grace is walking up to grab the first money bar, Jesse whispers to Max, "This is what you need to do; pull up her skirt, so everyone sees her underwear. It will be really funny, and everyone will laugh. You've got to do this."

Max says, "Hey, I am not sure. I don't want to do this. Isn't that mean?"

Jesse says, "No, I think Grace will think it's funny. She will be okay with it. Are you being a chicken?" And then he starts to make animal noises. *Cluck! Bawk!*

Once the chicken noises start, it puts Max over the edge. "Okay, I'll do it."

Smiling, Little Grace swings with ease from the first monkey bar to the second. I see Max from the corner of my eye; he's heading towards Grace. He raises his hands and pulls up Grace's skirt.

When that happens, immediately the crowd starts to chant, "Underwear, underwear, underwear, underwear…"

Little Grace is frozen; she does not know what to do. She feels trapped and mortified. *How can I get out of this situation?* Her brain is going a mile a minute, trying to figure out an exit. If she let's go of the bars, she will fall to the ground, and that will hurt. But if she keeps going, everyone will continue to look at her underwear and make fun of her.

Then the crowd starts to chant, "Blue-flowered underwear, blue-flowered underwear…" And of course, Jesse is the ringleader of it all.

Then he ups the ante. "Max, pull down her underpants, pull down her underpants…" The crowd starts chiming in again.

When Little Grace hears that, her hands get even more sweaty, and then she slips and falls to the ground. Everyone is laughing and mocking her; it seems to go on forever and ever. She is winded and can't even speak. She sits on the ground with her head down, hoping the taunting will end. They are now saying, "Grace is a crybaby. Such a crybaby, crybaby, crybaby…"

And Jesse says, "Boys are stronger than girls. Girls are weak. Look at her crying. Can't even do the monkey bars."

After what seems to be forever, the boys stop and move on to something else. There is nothing to see here anymore. All the fun is over for them.

Little Grace's knees are scraped from the fall. It is a minor wound when compared to the psychological one. I remember feeling embarrassed, scared, and betrayed. I knew that Little Grace was thinking, *How could Max do that to me? I thought he was my friend.*

What can I do for Little Grace now? How can I help her? I can see her shame. It penetrates her soul. Little Grace is ashamed of being a girl. She is regretful of putting herself in this situation. She wanted to be one of the boys and wishes she were at that moment, so she could fit in.

I watch Little Grace, remembering how I was paralyzed with terror and racking my brain for an escape. Her flight, fight, or freeze instinct kicked in. She froze, and I knew she couldn't reason her way out of the situation. I went through it myself; I experienced those feelings.

And now I'm triggered AGAIN. I feel the shame and terror once again. I am wounded again. I see now how that day impacted all my relationships. I never really got that when I was alive, even with therapy. I never felt like therapy worked. It was always rehashing things and never really resolving any issues. I guess I never realized how much this incident impacted me.

Like Little Grace, tears are streaming down my face. I realize now that I am still connected to my inner child. The fear and the sadness from that day still lies within me, and I'm aware of my brokenness. I never really did recover or heal from that experience. That day, I learned that boys are bad and that you can't ever trust them.

The anger came after that day. From that day forward, the trust was gone, replaced with disappointment. I lost my trust in Max, and I no longer trusted myself either. My world was changed. I think I lost my sense of self. In that moment, I detached from my femininity and toned down the softness for good.

It's clear now why I had to do that—for my own survival and protection. I felt weak and decided to shut down my vulnerability. Subconsciously, I built a wall around my heart so that I would never feel that same hurt and betrayal ever again. Max was part of it all, someone I loved, and my relationship with boys/men would never be the same.

Little Grace and Big Grace made their way home. Little Grace was afraid of what would happen when her mother saw her scraped knees. Grace would have to admit she went to the playground, and she would get in trouble. But she would never tell anyone what happened there. However, when Little Grace got back home, her parents hadn't even noticed she was gone. She climbed the stairs to the bathroom, cleaned off her knees, and then silently fled to her room.

I did everything to block that memory, stuff it down so low that it would never come to the surface for the next forty-two years, except for that stint in Tulum. I felt the same emotions at forty-two that I had at seven. The emotions were trapped in my body and were there throughout my life. It was not something that I was conscious of, but nonetheless they were still present. Even though many years had gone by, the same hurt, disappointment, and distrust permeated my dating life, boy after boy, man after man.

And the issue was even bigger than that. I felt that Little Grace had not defended her own honor. Questions of self-blame swirled in my mind. *Why didn't I protect myself? How could I let that happen? I decided to go to the playground, and I put myself in harm's way.*

I'm brought back to the present by Enzo. *Is there really a present when you are dead? Is everything the present when you are both seven and forty-two at the same time?*

I hear Enzo say, "Let's get the hell out of here now."

We are back in Central Park, in my happy place. Being surrounded by all the trees transforms my spirit. Most people don't know there are more than 20,000 trees in the park. The intense sadness, deep in my lungs, is ever so present; I can't catch my breath. Suddenly, I feel a jolt of healing energy; I'm not sure if it's coming from Enzo's superpowers or the beautiful rays of light from the sun. I feel a wall forming to protect my delicate heart. It is broken, just as it was when I was seven.

"Those boys are assholes. Screw them. This may make you feel better." Enzo hands me coffee. It's his way of taking care of me and expressing love.

I see in my hands a thick white mug filled with my favorite, the Americano. The aroma makes my heart sing and reminds me of Bluestone and one of my favorite pleasures as a live human. Enzo must have traded in some favors to make this happen because I got the impression he wasn't supposed to do things like this. He has gained some major points with me because I know this is his way of comforting me. Very touching. This sweetness is what I needed.

Normally, I would slough it off and disregard any kind gesture when I am in this kind of emotional state. But now, I am able to receive it fully. Being in spirit form, I experience the coffee in a different and new way. It isn't as though I need to eat and drink anymore; I mean, I *am* dead. My physical body is at least off the street, and now the gesture gives me a feeling of warmth and goodness, the same emotion I experienced when I drank the warm cup of goodness while sitting on my living-room lounger.

"Enzo! I thought you were watching your language."

"Oh shit. I was."

I laughed, and so did Enzo. We both knew he couldn't help himself. It will take him an infinity to master the art of appropriate language. Not his strong suit. Probably never will be. Remember, I am a realist.

"Grace, I'm so sorry. I feel for both you and Little Gracey. What betrayal and intense fear at an early age. And caused by someone you trusted and adored. I really am so sorry. Your loss of innocence and love. Throughout your life, you never really recovered. This is where your learning journey began, when you lost your openness, vulnerability, and trust. It's not only about loving others; it's about loving and accepting yourself. It's important that you witnessed this again to recognize when this began for you."

I'm quivering, tears streaming down my face. "I blocked that experience out for many years, and at one point, it came up in my late twenties. I went to intense therapy for it. I thought it was resolved. But it clearly wasn't because now I can still feel the intense pain and sadness. I wanted to save Little Grace, but I couldn't. As I was watching it all unfold again, I became paralyzed. It is as though I am seven years old again. That little girl is still feeling betrayed and is always searching for that love, the love and acceptance from a man. In my forty-two years, I never felt the intimacy that I longed for. Going back to my dating life and finding true love—is this what this journey is all about?"

"Well, not exactly, but I will say your openness and curiosity is a good start."

Where did he go? This popping in and out is confusing. What just happened here? Am I already starting a new task? Couldn't even finish my Americano. How does he do this? This is the superpower I want.

Focus, Grace.

Where am I headed now? I'm not sure I like this way of traveling. There's no control. When I was alive, I believed control was my superpower. But I guess not anymore.

♡

Exploration Questions
Chapter 3

Max and Jesse

1. How were you more fearless or less fearless as a child?

2. Who were your childhood playmates? Are you still in touch?

3. What are your favorite childhood memories? Riding your bike? Roller-skating?

4. What childhood hurt is still with you?

5. What patterns do you see in your relationships that are similar to those from your childhood?

Chapter 3 Activity

Reclaim Your Inner Child: Time travel a bit, and write a letter to your inner child. Tell her/him that you love her/him very much. Communicate that you are here to protect her/him and that you really appreciate who she/he is as a person. That you will honor and respect her/his needs. Then read the letter aloud slowly, and notice how you are feeling. It is okay to be sad or cry if you want to. Be real with your emotions, and let them out.

Chapter 4

Grayson

I find myself in front of a mirror and am taken aback at what I see. *Wait a minute. I look different. What is going on here?* I see a perplexed look in my reflection. Suddenly, the light bulb comes on, and I get it. This is what I looked like in my twenties. *Wow, I look quite young.* The hair is a bit weird, but that was the style twenty years ago—bangs with little waves on the sides. And not one gray hair peeking out of my scalp! I recently started to get more and more stragglers of gray hair right around my part. My reflection's hair has a few layers, but it's mainly straight and falls right below my shoulders. It is a little outdated now, but it was in style back then. I can't help admiring my clear and vibrant skin. My eyes are bright and full of possibility again, not dull and lifeless, as they were as I moved into my early forties.

I look around. *Where the hell am I?* I am clearly in someone's master bathroom. There are double sinks, a shower, and a soaking tub by the window. *Wow, this was the size bathroom I imagined I'd have when I got married and moved to the burbs. Let's check this place out.* My curiosity inspires me to wander.

I move into the next room, which is a huge master bedroom, definitely not my style of décor. The bedspread, carpeting, and window treatments are too farmhouse for me, not my contemporary chic style at all. The décor is a bit too traditional for my taste, although I am drawn to the grandness of the room and the tray ceiling. I don't remember being here before. I am hoping that something will spark my memory, maybe something outside. As I look out the window, I see a spacious yard, a stained-wood deck with patio furniture, a huge Weber grill, and a vast number of trees. It's beautiful, and I realize I am moved by all the nature surrounding me.

My thoughts are interrupted as Enzo pops up in front of me. I am still amazed by how he does that, just shows up out of nowhere.

"Ciao, you are at your next adventure! You don't seem thrilled."

That's correct; I am not. I am annoyed by his enthusiasm and over-zealous attitude. "Where am I? I have no clue why I am here and what I should be doing. I recognized the woods where you took me last time, but this place is foreign to me. I feel as though I don't belong here. Quite frankly, I am uncomfortable."

"No, you belong here. You were sent here on purpose. You will recognize the guy that lives here. The rest you don't know, and it won't matter. You need to relax and trust the process. Your role here is to help an old boyfriend. This is his family and his home. He is having a rough time in his marriage. You have been sent to assist in the matter. *Capisci?* Understand?"

"What? Are you kidding me here? I die right after a breakup, and now you are asking me to help an ex. Wow, that takes…guts."

Enzo smirked. "See, Grace, you are a quick study."

"Yeah, right. Don't mock me."

He nods his head, and, that fast, Enzo disappears.

I might as well take a look around and check out the place. I am in awe of how beautiful this home is. I find myself in a grand foyer with an elegant, yet simple, chandelier. To my right is a sitting room with a fireplace that is large enough for people to congregate around, yet cozy enough to read a book in front of with a cup of tea or even a glass of red wine. It doesn't feel lived in, though. The energy is flat, noticeably quiet. I peer into an adjoining room, which doesn't look any warmer. It must be the dining room, but it looks like it is used only for special holidays, like Christmas and Thanksgiving. In the room is a glass table that seats ten people and is a bit fancy, as compared to the rest of the home. Most of the furnishings are more of a colonial or country vibe. Although the table is chicer, more modern and Manhattan-like, which appeals to my style.

I move into the kitchen, which is in the back of the house. The tile floors would have echoed under my sturdy heels when I was alive. The kitchen is richly decorated with cherry cabinets, granite counter-tops, and a huge island surrounded by four stools. The sink is right near the window that looks out onto the beautiful backyard I saw from the upstairs window.

To the left, it looks like there is an office containing a grand dark-wood desk with a filing cabinet right next to it. Along the walls are custom built-ins filled with sports memorabilia, some from the New England Patriots, but mostly the shelves are filled with Red Sox items. Books of all shapes and sizes completely fill the rest of the shelves. There are two leather chairs facing one another with a round glass table in between them, coasters lying on its top. I can easily imagine a glass of red wine or even a Scotch resting on the table. Based on the décor of this man cave/office, it's hard to tell what the owner would prefer to drink.

I decide to regroup, so I sit down and lean back in the leather chair, trying to surmise where I am and what I am supposed to be doing here. Clearly, I was sent here for a reason, as Enzo mentioned. Although I am completely stumped at the moment.

"Who are you? And what are you doing in my daddy's office?"

Startled, I jump out of the chair. *Whoa! Where did she come from? Is she talking to me?* There is a little girl of about six, standing to my right, and if I didn't know better, I'd say she could see me. I didn't hear her coming as those tiny little feet marched across the thick carpeting. She is going to be in serious trouble when her mom sees that she has tromped across the rug in mud-squishy Keds.

"You can see me?"

She doesn't reply, but turns so fast that her pigtails snap in a semi-circle around her head as she runs from the room. She looks like a

GapKids model in her denim overalls and T-shirt. I can't tell if she is running because she is afraid of me or because she can't wait to tell on me.

I thought only Enzo could see me. *Who else can see me?* Or is this kid some kind of real-life Haley Joel Osment who can see dead people. I'm about to find out.

I sit back on the chair and yearn for an alcoholic beverage to numb this entire uncomfortable experience. Clearly, that is not going to happen, so I settle for a deep breath and imagine myself drinking a Pinot Noir in a Riedel glass.

Suddenly, the little girl is back again, but this time she brought someone with her. She is dragging an older man behind her and saying, "Daddy, Daddy, you have a visitor. Look, Daddy, look. Who is she?"

"Grayson?"

"Grace?! It can't be."

"Daddy…who is she?"

Barely able to get out a syllable, Grayson responds, "Olivia…Livy, this is an old friend of mine, Grace."

Old friend? Not so much. Totally not accurate. We were together for three and a half years and were not just friends. He almost proposed, but he is calling me his friend. I am now annoyed by his response. But then, almost immediately, I snapped out of it. It doesn't matter what he calls me now. Besides, you don't tell your kid you lived with someone other than Mommy.

Focus, Grace. Come back to the present.

The last thing I want is to scare the little girl, so I sit on the floor at the same level as Olivia and extend my hand. "Hi, Olivia, my name is Grace. It is nice to meet you."

Olivia responds with a bit of hesitancy, "Nice to meet you too."

Grayson looks toward the little girl. "Livy, thanks for letting me know that Grace is here. You can continue playing outside in the backyard."

"Okay, Daddy." She races outside and stops close to the window, through which I can see her writing in the dirt with a small twig, seemingly unfazed by finding me in her father's study. She is engrossed in the present; kids are good like that. She probably already forgot all about me.

Grayson and I lock eyes. He is speechless, which is quite common for him. Happened quite a bit when we were dating. He once had to take a Myers-Briggs personality test as part of a leadership class. He always dreaded attending those classes since he would have to talk in front of others about his areas of development. The personality test revealed an ISTJ response. Grayson scored as an exceedingly high I and J, introverted and judgmental. Yeah, that was fun to date. Very rigid and didn't say too much. Not an easy combination when it comes to communicating. We would go on a weeklong vacation, and he would read as many as five books during what was supposed to be a romantic getaway. I would get bored and end up swimming by myself or walking along the shore to do some shelling to keep myself occupied. What was the point of traveling with someone who always kept to himself? It emphasized the differences between us.

Finally, he speaks and gets a sentence out. "Grace, what are you doing here? I thought you were dead. I heard from Tom Demeter that you died a couple of weeks ago. Hit by a car in Manhattan. Did he get that wrong? He said he read it on Facebook."

"No, Grayson. Tom got it right. I'm dead."

"No, you're not. You're standing right in front of me. How is this plausible? Was it somebody else with the same name?"

Oh my God, how do I convince somebody I'm dead? I know. Am I solid? Can he put his hand through me? Ew.

"If you are dead, did you see the white light? Did it hurt? Were you looking down at people? Did you see God?"

"None of the above. But I saw everyone surround my body on the street. And then I was greeted by a guide named Enzo."

"Enzo, well that is quite an Italian name. Not one of the apostles—Mark, Matthew, Luke, or John? Did he greet you with a slice of pizza?"

"Very funny and you are stereotyping a bit."

"Well, Grace, how do I know that this is really you?"

"Okay, then ask me a question that only I would know."

"When we were on vacation in Aruba, what was the name of your dolphin when we swam with the dolphins?"

"Gabriel."

"Okay, one more question with that trip in mind. What was the name of the horse you rode when we went horseback riding?"

"Harrison Ford. Any other questions?"

"I guess not. You answered them without hesitation. Boy, that's a rough way to go." He paused and then said, "Which I was deeply sorry to hear, by the way."

"Grayson, I know this is all so strange. Trust me, it is hard for me to make heads or tails of it. An angel—I guess you wouldn't call him that. A guide told me that I am here to help you in some way. Not sure in what capacity I am here to provide this support and guidance, but here I am. Through this experience, I am supposed to be helping you and me. It is a joint effort here. What are you going through personally?"

"I want it to hear it from him."

There's got to be a problem because I am here. Isn't it the case, though, that in order to be open to support, people must first admit that they need help?

Grayson changes the subject. "Grace, you look the way I remember you—your hair, your face—and you are in that black Providence College sweatshirt you would wear on my couch when we were watching TV together."

I look down and say, "Yeah, I loved this sweatshirt. Not sure what happened to it after we broke up. And now here it is. I am not sure why I am here, either. But this is where I have been sent. I know it has been a while, about ten years, since we last spoke."

"That's about right. So what are you doing in my house? And I still don't understand how Livy and I can see you. You did die, didn't you? You are not here to come haunt me now, are you?"

I was losing patience by the minute with his stupid questions. "Grayson, get over yourself. I did die, and now my eternity is not all about hanging with you. The sooner you clean up your act, the quicker you are rid of me. By the way, your daughter is cute. She has your eyes."

He then softened and became less afraid. "Thank you. She is one of my greatest gifts in life, and I'm thankful for her every day. So…how are we going to figure out why you are here, in my home?" He always went back to the task at hand.

"No clue at this moment. But I am sure it will get clearer, and I will let you know as soon as I know."

I look down at my sweatshirt and remember those lazy nights on the couch. I really did love him. He was stable, reliable, and punctual. He always paid the check when we were out to dinner and held open the door, but I felt alone when I was in his company. Grayson was there physically, but checked out mentally and emotionally. As I mutter these words, I put my hand on my heart and…

I'm back by the Reservoir in Central Park. *Do I have this superpower now?* This must mean check-in time with Enzo. I wouldn't mind sitting on a couch right now, an Americano in my hand. Better yet, Enzo could at least bring me a cappuccino.

"Hi, Grace! So I am taking it that you figured out whose house it is. Am I right?"

"You're laughing? You think this is funny? Every ten minutes, I snap into a new location. This is exhausting. And terrifying!"

"And how is it to be back wearing your favorite sweatshirt? I felt that was a nice touch to mark that time when you dated Grayson. Back to the comforts of home for you, except all you are missing are those baggy gray Adidas sweatpants you wore constantly. Those died a long time ago, and I was not bringing them back!"

Finally, Enzo picks up on the fact I am not happy. "So what's on your mind, Grace?"

My mind is stewing, and I am not thrilled by the entire situation. "I don't know what to do. And then—poof!—I arrive at his house and am being greeted by his daughter. I have not seen him in ten years, and I now know he has moved on in his beautiful house, with his adorable daughter, and I am sure his wife is perfectly all the things I wasn't."

Enzo senses this is not good. This conversation was going down a rabbit hole, so he quickly changes trajectory. "Is that jealousy I'm hearing in your voice? Regret maybe? If I remember correctly, in the end you were clear that he was not the man for you. He may have been a season for you, but not a lifetime. And, Grace, that was the right decision for both him and you. He knows it, and deep down so do you."

That statement stopped me in my tracks. The obsessing ended. "Yeah, you are right. I never wanted to admit it, and I was so hesitant to take the next step, which was engagement and then marriage. I felt bad in the end because I knew that was what he wanted, but my gut told me that we were not right for each other in the long term. I was afraid to be alone again and invested so much time and energy in that relationship. I knew I was going to have my heart broken over it and didn't want to experience that. The truth is, I was the one who initiated the breakup. Not Grayson. Something was not right about it.

He was perfect on paper, but when we were together, we didn't always connect. I felt alone with him. I not only caused his heartbreak, but my own as well. So I don't understand why now I am reunited with him. Any insight or details you'd like to share with me?"

"As I said in the beginning, I'm not supposed to give you a ton of direction, although this experience can provide healing and support for both of you. And you are the one that will be leading it; you have the capacity and skills to help him and, in the end, help yourself."

My cynical and sarcastic attitude kicked in and was in full command. "Are you kidding me? I am supposed to help him? Help him what? What about me? You are telling me that my peace and transformation is dependent on Grayson. On Earth, I was with him for three and a half years. Are you now saying that I have to spend my eternity supporting him? What?! This is bullshit. I could not help him while we were together for those years. What makes you—or whoever is upstairs—think I can do this now? Do I have some sort of new superpower? Or are we going for a full-on miracle?"

Enzo gave me his tough-love look and said, "Yes, Grace. Yes. You need to put your big-girl pants on. Right now."

Whoosh!

I find myself back in Grayson's study, in the same leather chair where I first encountered Livy and Grayson.

Grayson walks into the room, and when he sees me sitting there, he is not as weirded out as he was before. "Oh, you're back."

"Try not to sound so thrilled, Grayson."

"It was not a dream that Olivia and I were experiencing. And I guess I am not losing it. I have been super stressed at work, and now that's working its way into my personal life, especially with my wife, Amy. Lately, I have had zero patience, and I'm taking it out on the kids a little bit, but mostly on Amy. I don't really appreciate all that she does around the house. She did leave her career to raise our children. I know that was a hard decision for her to make."

I say, "Happy wife, happy life."

"Well, I will say that my marriage is not going well. I've been trying to figure out how and why you are here. And, somehow, I feel a bit of relief as I am confessing it to you, Grace. This is the first time I am saying it out loud. As you know, I am not one to share my feelings; I keep things close to the vest. I hate gossip, but since you're dead, I guess you are not a real person, so it is okay to share it."

What does he mean I am not a 'real person'?

Grayson continues to share, "What I don't get is how calm Amy is in general. Deep down, I wish that she would be a little unglued at times, maybe scream and yell. It would make me feel better about my inadequacies when it comes to dealing with pressure."

He continues, "Did you figure out why you are here? I think it came to me. A week ago, I walked into a church on Sunday. It was a Sunday afternoon between church services. I did go in and kneel in the first pew. I looked up at Jesus on the Cross and said out loud, 'God, I need help. Please help me some way, some how.' And here you are. Although we didn't work out, and you have had your fair share of failed relationships. So how will our meeting again help my situation?"

"Ouch, that stung." I am annoyed with his flippant attitude. Sometimes he was so insensitive and operated in his head too much. It was as though he was completely disconnected from his feelings. I laugh to myself. Some things haven't changed. It was a good thing that we did not get married.

I took a deep breath and started to share all that happened since our monumental breakup night. The one major plus with Grayson is that he is, in fact, quite a good listener…when he isn't attached to his devices or watching the television. And he *was* sharing a bit about his marriage, so I guess that there's been some growth.

Grayson's eyes welled up with tears, and he said in an octave-higher pitch that was filled with anxiety, "Grace, you are here to help me save my marriage."

And there it was—his truth. With wide eyes and an even fuller understanding of the gravity of the situation, I said, "I'll do my best to help."

I feel a strong need to hug Grayson, but I'm not sure if that would be breaking any rules. He's married, and I'm dead. I decide against it. No hug.

Grayson said, "I need help. I don't know what to do. I find solutions all the time at work, and here I am now. I got nothing. Maybe God answers prayers in the most mysterious ways."

When I knew him, he was always about solving the problem, which was both a blessing and a curse. Sometimes, people just needed him to be present and available so that they could talk to him. He never really understood the value of the times when he truly listened. It was his secret superpower and one that lately, from how he was describing himself at home, he was not using much. Things were getting bleaker; he felt the distance between him and his wife Amy. At this juncture, it seemed he was open to—or more like desperate for—the help. Which is not usual for him. It was different for me to see him this way.

Grayson asked all the questions within seconds, "So how do we get started? Do you approach Amy? Will she be able to see you? Do you move stuff around, like in that Demi Moore movie? Wasn't it called *Spirit*? No, it was *Ghost*. That's it. Or try to get in her mind to see what she is thinking? What are your ideas?"

After a minute, I put a halt to his 21 Questions; he was stressing me out already. He never spoke this much when we were together, even when we were away on a weeklong trip. *Wow, he's changed a bit and is more engaged. Why didn't he show more of this side when we were together?* "Wait a minute here. I might be dead, but I am not a mind reader. And if Amy saw me, what do you think she would do? How much did you share about us…or me? Not a winning combination to say you are talking about your crumbling marriage to your dead ex-girlfriend. Let's be smart about this. Our focus is *not* to get you divorced here."

I saw the light bulb go off in his head. Grayson comprehended what he had been saying, so he changed his tune a bit. "Grace, you have a good point. She would freak out if she saw you, which would not help matters here."

"How about you reenergize your connection with Amy. The feelings were there at some point; they can be again. Maybe take some time off from work to devote yourself to her and your marriage without any distractions. When's the last time you spent time with Amy…alone?"

"Well, um…oh… Okay, I can't seem to remember right now."

I followed up with, "Exactly. Maybe it's time to make time for you and Amy. Get back the spark, the feeling that brought you both together. A romantic evening, perhaps?"

I can see he's mulling it over and not entirely convinced it will work, but my idea is probably better than doing nothing. Or wasting more time to come up with a better plan.

"Okay, I'll make a reservation. I know the place. I'll see what I can do to make it happen."

Ordinarily, this would be the moment that I asked Grayson to pour me a big glass of red wine from my favorite winemaker, the Prisoner. It was a bit pricey, but well worth it. With the pressure of having to figure out how to help Grayson move forward with this delicate situation, the wine may have calmed my nerves a bit. I would settle for the Predator—a little less expensive, but tasty. But I will just have to do this sober. Sometimes death really sucks. Now I feel responsible for Grayson…and Amy too. *What has Enzo gotten me into?! This is already harder than I anticipated!*

Grayson is suddenly gone, and in his place, Enzo appears, right here in the study. He must be somewhere inside my brain, somehow wired into each thought I have. It is a bit annoying and borderline creepy.

"You rang?"

I swear he looks devious for an angel. Aren't they supposed to be nice, or, I don't know, angelic? "How do you do that? Know that I need your assistance or am thinking about you."

"What? It creeps you out, Grace?" Enzo then winks.

"Yes!"

"Look, Grace, energy is powerful. In my role, one of my superpowers is to sense energy. That is what I can offer you as support. I know that one of the things you were always looking for was a man who really showed up for you. Maybe you had that a bit with your dad or grandfather, but not with an intimate partner. I am here now for you. I am showing you that people do show up in your life. You are independent, you wanted to do everything yourself, and you had success that way…to a point. It is about accepting others' help and what they have to give. Don't do this alone. Let's face it; letting people help you is very hard for you. The thing you wanted most was the thing that you couldn't receive. You are worthy. I am here and available to you, no matter what. I am showing you what you wanted, so you can experience it. Are you in a place to receive it now? That is the real task at hand."

"Why are we bringing him back to me again? We have a crisis here, and now I am responsible for saving my ex-boyfriend's marriage. That is a little f—cked up, don't you think? I already paid my dues with him."

"Let's refocus here, Grace. This is all about you and your learning. Amy and Grayson, and even little Livy, are just in your world; it is your experience."

"Okay, let's get back to the task at hand. What can I do here? Grayson is Grayson—not sure how much I can change that. I couldn't do it back when we were dating. What makes you think I can do it now?"

"Yes, you can't change him. That is his responsibility. So what is in your control? How can you help the situation?"

Well, let me think about this… "My feeling is that they have not had alone time in a while, so maybe it is about getting them to connect again without the kids. Just the two of them. I am good at helping women get ready for dates. God knows, I have a lot of practice in that department, with my own love life. And maybe I can help Grayson be a bit more romantic. He falls a bit short in that area. It is about creating that spark that I know they once had in the beginning. Getting them to remember why they got together in the first place. Hmm, so where do I start?"

♡

Exploration Questions
Chapter 4

Grayson

1. In your life, are there relationships in which you held a grudge? What was the impact of that on you and on others?

2. Have you ever held on to a piece of clothing or some other item from an ex? If yes, what was it? What made you hold on to it? Do you still have it?

3. Which one of your exes would you help and why?

4. How do you think a friend or ex would react if you popped back in as a ghost?

5. How important is date night to a couple?

Chapter 4 Activity

Acknowledge Affirmations of Love: Sit or stand in front of a mirror, and tell yourself, "I am enough." Use other affirmations, such as "I am strong" or "I stand up for myself" or "I am beautiful" or "I am worthy" or other "I am" statements that are important to you. You can post these phrases where you can see them every day...as friendly reminders!

Chapter 5

The Closet

I am standing in so much space. In my time in Manhattan, I never had as much closet space as I am experiencing here. I can dance in this space and all this room for shoes! Let me peek outside the door. Now it is coming back to me. I've been in this bedroom before.

I was glad that I convinced Grayson. Got him to make date night with Amy a priority. No kids or work. Time for them to talk, laugh, and connect. An opportunity for them to relive the magic and rekindle the love that first brought them together.

Oh, this must be Amy's closet. I knew I was sent here for a reason; my first task is to find something fabulous for Amy to wear on her big date with Grayson. There must be something in this closet that is simple yet sexy. Nothing that she would wear to a school function or soccer game. Amy needs to look beautiful. Yes, it was partly for Grayson, for him to be attracted and excited. I feel for Amy. I want her to feel desirable and beautiful on the date.

I only knew of Amy, have never met her face-to-face, but I heard a while back she had married Grayson. A mutual college friend told me about his engagement. She didn't even tell me on purpose. She was talking about it, and I guess she thought I already knew. She was going on and on about how nice Amy was and what a good fit Grayson and she were. I have to say it stung a bit. I know we broke up, but in some ways, I still felt replaced and easily substituted. Plus, at the time I was single, so I didn't have the distraction of being in a new loving, intimate relationship. I was alone, and Grayson had moved on happily. I acted as if I were excited for him, but it was just a front; deep down it triggered some sadness. Sadness that I did not know I had within me.

And then, two years later, I heard from that same friend that he had his first child, and again that elicited the same feeling of melancholy. I had been so sure that I would start a family before Grayson, but that was not the case. I am not even sure why I kept talking to that mutual friend, since she always updated me on Grayson's life. At the time, I wanted to know about him, but just as soon as I heard something, I regretted the update because it made me aware that Grayson was living his best life without me.

Now back to scanning the clothing in Amy's closet. She needs some serious help here. Amy must have something in here besides navy-blue suits from Brooks Brothers and work dresses from Talbots. I could see her style was on the conservative side. I am impressed by how organized this closet is—work attire on one side and casual on the other. Not so many shoes, besides her sneakers and flip-flops. Where are the heels and the boots? She does live in New England. I see snow boots and UGGs, but what about the staple of a black-leather boot? Okay, so I am not in Manhattan anymore, but not even a brown pair? Wow, this may be a bit more challenging than I first expected. A lot of these clothes are outdated. I see no new tags or clothing that has a fun vibe. It is all about corporate in this closet. I thought she stayed at home. This closet could use a good decluttering by using the KonMari method to create more space for clothes that she will actually wear and that bring her joy.

This is not my problem to solve; let's stick to the task at hand. Okay, what do we have here…? No, to this side of the closet. Let me reach towards the back of it.

"Aha! Okay, this we can work with!" Whew, I was starting to get nervous about finding something, and I usually can work with most items.

It was one of my essential duties for Hope, my number one bestie, but her taste in clothing was a bit all over the place. She always got a bit stressed about what item to wear on a first date. I would come over and see what she was thinking, and then choose another option. Bless her soul, but picking out outfits was not her strong suit. I adore that one and miss her. She would get a kick out of me right now, having to self-reflect and go through this in order to complete my time here on Earth. Hope bought me so many journals; I wrote in each one, at least a page or two, but then got distracted and forgot about them, leaving them to collect dust in my drawer.

Ah yes, this is the dress! It's a one-sleeved black cocktail dress by Vince Camuto. Why this gem is hidden way in the back—behind the sea of blue suits that are items she hasn't worn in years and at this point are out of style—I do not know. *Okay, now I have to find shoes to match...and also a bag. And let's not forget her jewels.*

Wait a minute! I am no longer alone. Who's with me? I wish I had X-ray vision, or at least some prior knowledge when I am about to be greeted by someone. I would think I would have inherited that ability, like the boy in *The Sixth Sense*. He could sense all spirits around him. I really loved that movie, especially the scene when he tells his mother the truth and what happened to the bumblebee pendant.

Ahh, this is Amy. I guess she cannot see me, which is different than Grayson and her daughter Olivia. She's a good fit for Grayson. Very natural, no makeup, and her hair up in a ponytail. I get the appeal, and she is definitely his type. Nothing overdone or fake, more on the plain side, more real. A better match than I was, which makes me sad and evokes regrets. Not sure why I am feeling this way. I was the one who let the relationship go. This could have been my house and my family.

It is a beautiful house, although it's not my style. And seeing that they are struggling doesn't draw me to this lifestyle. It is hard to raise a family and make a marriage work. I guess I always felt marriage would save me from loneliness. But Amy and Grayson don't seem connected. Actually, I feel a bit sad for them. They have everything—big house, healthy children—but they seem to have lost what brought them together.

Amy needs a night out in which she feels appreciated and loved. As I approached my forties, I discovered the wisdom that every woman deserves to get all dressed up and feel good. To shine with the beauty from within and let their external view match that internal glow. There's no feeling like it—seeing your magnificence as you stand before a full-length mirror. Unfortunately, it was a rare occasion in my life when I could both feel and see my own radiance. I was looking outside of myself for that validation. I can see now how that never served me.

Let's get back to the task at hand. She's in the closet now. Okay, so I need her to see this dress. I can't hand it to her; there has to be a way for it to grab her attention. She can't see me, but I can take the dress off the hanger and throw it on the floor.

Good idea, Grace! So here goes nothing.

The dress falls to the floor. I knew that move would catch Amy's eyes, and indeed she looks at the puddle of black on the floor. Amy picks up the dress and holds it directly against her body. Then she turns from her reflection in the mirror, all proud. Smiling, she says out loud in the closet, "This is it; this is the one."

Mission accomplished. But I am still not finished here. I need to continue to support Amy in her makeover for the upcoming date. Aha! Amy will need a blowout of some sort. The hair in the ponytail won't do justice to her thick, full head of brownish-red hair. Somehow, I need to make Amy think of the idea. I can tell she probably never does this for herself and thinks of it as a wasted expense.

I always used to get frustrated with my friends who were Moms. They always put themselves last when, quite frankly, they deserved to be put at the front of the line. *Self-care* was a word lacking from their vocabulary. They deserved the absolute best. It was important for them to make the time and spend the money to invest in their own physical, emotional, and mental well-being. They got shortchanged.

I became such an advocate of spa treatments, yoga classes, long weekends with girlfriends, and anything else that would elevate their spirits.

I am one to talk. There were times I was working late nights, burning the midnight oil, waking up with bags under my eyes, and making self-care a "wouldn't it be lovely." Okay, I guess I was a bit of a hypocrite.

After seeing the dress, Amy is still perplexed by how it got on the floor since her closet was fairly organized.

Something draws Amy to the dresser with the jewelry box on top of it. She says out loud, "I guess I should wear some jewelry. Wow, I am out of practice at getting dressed up. Because of the style of the neckline, there's no need for a necklace, but earrings are in order. Okay, these are the ones." She picks a pair of diamond-mosaic drop earrings in fourteen-karat white gold.

From the bottom row of her jewelry box, Amy chose a David Yurman classic cable bangle. As Amy studies her reflection, her facial expression changes instantly. That beaming, confident smile at finding "the" dress turns into a frown of disgust as she touches her hair. "What a mess! My hair is dreadful!" she mumbles as her shoulders sink towards the floor.

I've got the solution—the Miraculous Blowout. Based on seeing Amy in person and the items in her closet, I got the sense that Amy did not do things for herself. I bet she saw it is an extravagant expense since she was home with the children and not bringing in a salary. I needed to intervene here and encourage her to schedule that blowout. Earlier, I had seen a coupon from a local salon downstairs; I quickly retrieved it and then placed it right on her dresser so she could see it. It read, "For first-timers, enjoy a blowout for only $30.00 for any style and length of hair. Please check us out!" That's a price that Amy will probably be comfortable with.

In that moment, Amy noticed the coupon and said, "Okay, seeing this is a sign."

Amy picked up her phone, tapped some keys, listened, and then said, "Yes, I'd like to make an appointment for a blowout on Friday at 4:00 p.m. I have a coupon here; it says the price is $30 for first-timers. Are you still honoring it? Okay, yes, then I will see you at 4:00 p.m. on Friday. Thank you."

And I thought to myself, *My work is done for now. Game on!*

♡

Exploration Questions
Chapter 5
The Closet

1. Have you met or do you know the partner of an ex? How do you get along?

2. When you get ready to go out, for whom do you dress?

3. What do you think about the concept that a partner "completes you"?

4. In what ways do you practice self-care daily?

5. How can you accept your life and be at peace when things are not going according to plan?

Chapter 5 Activity

Clean Out Your Closet: Now is the time to go through your closet and remove anything that doesn't make you feel good about yourself. Time to let go of the old and make space for the new!

Chapter 6

Amy and Grayson

It was Friday at 5:30 p.m., officially the big date night for Amy and Grayson. The kids were running around in the basement, excited as Amy told them Emily, their babysitter, was coming over and would be playing games with them all night.

Grayson was in his study, already dressed and ready to go. He looked nervous as he sat in his office quietly sipping on a Scotch. He started whispering, "Grace, Grace, where are you? Grace, I need to talk with you? Grace, Grace, I thought you were going to help me tonight?"

I still don't understand how I now show up precisely at the right moment, when I was never punctual while alive. I usually arrived about ten minutes late for most meetings and functions. I got away with it because people liked to be around me, so I guess they accepted my lack of punctuality. What a mystery this new time and space is. I still don't get how it works.

I am hoping that I am doing the right thing here. I definitely don't want to stay in this space forever. I'm in limbo—one foot in the living world and the other one in the afterlife. It's exhausting being in transition. Everyone needs to land and feel that they are at home. And that includes *moi*! Even if temporary and short-lived, people deserve a sense of security and comfort. Luckily, I only moved once while growing up, and when I did, it was dreadful. There's no fun in being the "new girl." Too much attention, especially from the people you don't want to notice you.

"I'm here. What's the panic? What's up? Are you ready?" I look him up and down. "Is that what you are wearing?" *Oh no!*

Grayson has on a wrinkled, gray, collared, casual polo shirt, which at least is tucked in with a brown belt, jeans that are worn at the knees, and brown loafers. He responds with a perplexed look on his face, "No good? These are my lucky jeans, so comfortable. And let's face it, Grace; I could use a little luck tonight."

"Hell no, those jeans need to go to clothing heaven. You need to change; this is what you would wear at your son's soccer game. Tonight is about reconnecting with your wife, so you need to put a little thought into it. Okay, go back upstairs, and find something else, maybe a button-down. Make sure it is pressed. No jeans and nicer shoes. You can do better. Jazz it up a bit here. Try to make an effort."

Grayson's shoulders slumped in that defeated husband look, but he dutifully headed back upstairs.

About thirty minutes later, I am thinking, *Where is he?* I am wondering what he will come up with. *How many clothes does he have? Why is this taking so long?*

Grayson finally walks back into the room. He has on a crisp blue button-down, black pressed slacks, a stylish Brooks Brothers black belt, and black dress shoes. He's holding a gray Ralph Lauren sports coat. He even put a little gel in his hair. With a bashful look and his eyes focused on the floor, he asks, "Is this okay?"

Wow, this brings me back to a memory of one the dates we had. It was our first anniversary, and he showed up at my apartment door in a blue sports coat, khaki pants, and white button-down shirt, carrying a bouquet of flowers. Seeing him, I really fell for him hard.

Looking at Grayson now, even with a little less hair and a few gray strands, he still is as handsome as ever. I am taken aback and try to regain my composure. "Yep, that will do." I don't want to let on that in this moment I am a bit smitten with him. *Why am I feeling this way?*

It is long over, he is married, and I'm dead. Not to mention I am supporting his wife. Rooting for Amy. *Let's keep on task, Grace.*

"Are you getting Amy flowers?"

Grayson fumbles a bit with his words and finally says, "Oh, I didn't realize. I didn't think about that. Okay, let me jump in the car and get some." And in a dash, he is out the door.

Meanwhile, I am watching Amy put on her finishing touches. Amy looks at her blown-out hair in the mirror. She beams and says, "Why don't I do this more often? My hair looks fantastic!" She puts on her jewelry, and even some eye shadow.

Amy looks at herself in the mirror and says, "Breathe, Amy. Just have a good time; don't overanalyze it. And don't put pressure on yourself or Grayson. Just be…"

Amy took one more deep breath and headed toward the stairs.

Now I am feeling the pressure. They both seem so anxious. In my current state, I can feel so much more now within myself and the emotions around me. I guess this is the entire point of my being here—accessing these emotions. I used to be able to escape them by going straight into my mind and picking up a new book. I can see that was somewhat of an escape mechanism.

Grayson pulls back in the driveway. I greet him at the car and say, "Amy is ready. Go to the front door."

Grayson questions, "The front door? I always come through the garage."

"Seriously, do you want my help or not? Just trust me on this. And I will be on your date to support you. I will only chime in when you need my assistance. And I'll know when to intervene. Don't mess this up, Grayson. No pressure." And then I smile at him.

Amy starts down the stairs and is greeted by big smiles from Olivia and Ryan. Ryan blurts out, "Wow, Mom, you look so beautiful. Dad is going to like you."

Livy says, "Mom, you are so pretty. Your hair looks different."

Amy blushes a bit and then acknowledges the kind words. "Thanks, Ryan and Livy. You going to be good for Emily and have fun?"

Ryan rolls his eyes. "Yes, Mom, we will."

Grayson walks through the door as Amy is heading down the stairs. He looks taken aback by how dressed up Amy is, but collects himself as little Livy tugs on his pants.

She says, "Doesn't Mommy look pretty?"

He responds, "She is exceptionally beautiful. Daddy is an incredibly lucky man," as he approaches Amy, takes her arm, and leads her out the front door.

They arrive at the restaurant—or should I say that we all arrived at the restaurant, because I seem to pop up there just as they walk in the door. It is a small Italian place in town—round tables with white tablecloths, a single white rose in a bud vase, and a bottle of olive oil. It's not easy to get a reservation on a Friday night, especially at a small neighborhood place, like this, with only seven tables. The food is always good at these simple, elegant spots. Grayson must know the owner to get this last-minute reservation.

Before they go in, Grayson pulls the red roses from the back seat of the car and says, "These are for you."

Amy is clearly touched by the kind gesture. "Thank you, they are beautiful."

Grayson says, "Like my wife. You look hot in that dress."

Amy musters up a bashful smile and says in a low voice while avoiding eye contact, "Thanks."

As they walk through the front doors, the maître d' greets them with a smile. "Hello. My name is Marco. I am here to help while Matteo is in Italy, visiting his mother. I am one of his many cousins," chuckling a bit as he speaks the words. "Please sit down, here at the back table, facing the window. Matteo told me this is your favorite spot."

Once they get to their table, Grayson hands Marco both their coats and then pulls the chair out so Amy can sit down and get settled in at the table. Then Grayson follows suit and sits down next to Amy.

I think, *Good move, Grayson, you are doing well so far, very attentive. Keep it up.*

In about a minute, Marco is back asking, "Would you like water? Sparkling or tap?"

In unison, they both say, "Yes, tap."

"Great, tap it is. Are you celebrating an anniversary or birthday?"

Grayson spoke up first and said, "No, it's just been a while since we have been out together." At that moment, he grabs Amy's hand.

Grayson never was much of a romantic; he is trying, really trying here.

As Marco is reapproaching the table with the water, a series of beeps emanates from Grayson's sports coat. He is trying to ignore it, but he starts to fidget a bit. Instead of answering the phone, he attempts to concentrate on Amy and engage in a conversation.

Amy must know that look on Grayson's face well. "Do you need to get that?"

Grayson stutters a bit, indicating he knows he shouldn't answer the call, but he gives in anyway. "Let me check it. I promise I'll be back in five minutes." Grayson then stands and walks away from the table.

I throw my arms up in exasperation. I get it, sole breadwinner of the family. I'm sure he is under a lot of pressure. *But, come on, one night, Grayson. Stay off the phone for just an hour, will you?*

Amy gets Marco's attention, looks at the wine list, and points to a Sangiovese. She says under her breath, "I might as well get a good glass of wine out of this dinner. And I am going for the best bottle."

I can see the look of disappointment and sadness in Amy's eyes, and now I am pissed. After a strong start, Grayson is going downhill very quickly. Same old pattern—I guess some things don't change.

I need to intervene. I mean, that's why I'm here, to help bail out my ex, and it's bringing up some feelings of resentment left over from when I was dating Grayson.

I find Grayson pacing the sidewalk in front of the restaurant, deep in conversation, and I hear snippets of "client...contract...deadline..." Without thinking, I smack the phone out of his hand, and it goes crashing to the pavement. *Wow, anger seems to make me powerful.*

Grayson yells, "What are you doing? That phone is expensive, and I need it for work."

I have to actually scream some sense into him. "What am I doing? Saving your ungrateful ass. The real question is, what are *you* doing? You are blowing this entire date. You can't even give Amy, the mother of your children, one evening of your attention. I thought you were committed to doing whatever it takes to save this marriage. Actions speak louder than words, Grayson.

"And quite frankly, this is how I felt in our relationship. You were always focused on work. Everything and everyone always came second. Sometimes I did not even make it to third place. Your inability to take the time to build and focus on us was the demise of our relationship. I always felt like a chore to you, that it was an inconvenience to spend time with me. When I met you, you were building your career; that was your priority.

"Now you have been at that firm for how long? And you are still giving them most of your energy and time. What about your family? What about your relationship with Amy? What happens when all that goes to shit? What regrets will you have then?"

"Grace, you don't understand. I am responsible for two children and a wife...and have a large mortgage. We can't afford for me not to take these client calls or not to respond to my boss."

"Sure, but at what cost? All your children and wife want is for you to be engaged and to be present for them. That is what the kids will remember. 'Did I spend time with Dad? Was it quality time? Did I have fun with him?' In the end, it is not about living in a fancy house."

In that moment, Grayson forgot about the phone, which was lying cracked on the pavement.

"Picture yourself twenty years down the road. What kind of relationship do you have with your kids? Do you have any idea what is going on in their lives, what is important to them? Will you even still be married to Amy?"

He doesn't respond.

"Grayson, Grayson. What are you going to do now? It's your choice."

"Go back inside and have dinner with my wife."

"You better start baring your soul and being honest about where you are at. That will save you. Otherwise, your relationship is heading down the road of destruction. You will lose her."

I follow him back into the restaurant.

Grayson sits down and apologizes immediately, "Amy, I am sorry that I took the call and left the table." She is visibly upset because she is avoiding eye contact.

Something comes over Amy; she looks right at Grayson and starts erupting like a volcano, except instead of hot lava coming out of her mouth, the words she must have had bottled up for years begin to flow. The wine is kicking in and loosening her tongue. "Grayson, I thought tonight was supposed to be about us. It never is anymore. All your energy is given to your job and then the kids. Where am I in this equation? Well, I'll tell you where I am. I fall in last place. Here I thought if I wore a sexy dress, put some makeup on, and got my hair done that I could keep your attention for at least the length of dinner. We didn't even get to appetizers. I ordered a bottle of wine. I ordered it myself because you were outside, busy with work, for fifteen minutes. I am sitting here alone at the table, feeling like such an idiot. And now I have no appetite, and I've wasted money on a perfectly good blowout. Let's go. Date over." Amy reaches for her purse and heads out the door.

Grayson begs, "Please, please, Amy. Let's stay. Look, I am sorry. I know I have been an insensitive ass lately. I am so stressed about work and being a good provider for you, for the kids. Things have not been the same with us. I haven't been present or emotionally available. I am not good at that. I'm not sure that I have ever been that guy. I don't know how to do this."

With tears in her eyes, Amy says, "I feel like you used to be there and wanted to be with me. The first couple of years, you showed me through acts of kindness. You would warm up the car for me, bring me my favorite scone from the local bakery, and plan a fun adventure with me at least once a month. It is all about the little things that you did. Now, with all your free time, you go into your study and close the door. It is as though you have to escape from the kids, from me. I don't want to live like this, like we are roommates, talking only when we need to arrange a soccer game or a play date.

"Growing up, I was never certain that I would be a mother, or was even capable of being one. But when I met you, I had this feeling of possibility. A feeling that together we would make a good team. That I could raise a family with you. Now I feel all by myself, totally alone in this. Even when you are there, you are not really there. I am afraid that we are not going to make it." In that moment, Amy stops and the look on her face shows that she is surprised by everything she has just said. But I do not see regret there. Maybe relief?

Grayson felt defeated and scared. "Okay, let's go." He asked for their coats and handed Amy's to her as she walked through the front door.

They headed back to the car in silence.

This situation was very familiar, and it triggered something in me. It brought me back to the moment that I knew it was over with Grayson. We were on the front steps of my apartment. I walked inside, and he drove away, never to connect again…until now—or more precisely, two days ago—when we saw each other in his study.

After they got home, Amy walked in and straight upstairs. The bedroom door clicked shut, and I heard muffled crying.

Grayson sat down on the front steps, breathing in the fresh, crisp air. He looks up and sees me glaring at him. "Yeah, I know. I blew it. We couldn't last the entire date. It's not good."

"What do you mean, *we*, Grayson? *You* blew it. Amy showed up. She was present and focused only on you. She wasn't on the phone with the babysitter, was she?"

He suddenly had a flashback of a similar conversation he had on front steps. Grayson made the connection. "Oh my God, this is what happened to us. Different relationship, yet same issues. I shut you out, didn't I?"

I took a deep breath, paused, and answered, "Yes."

"I was on a high-profile project and working long hours, completely attached to my Blackberry at the time. Thinking about it, I was not around. I was more committed to the job. I thought you would have a good time anyway, whether I accompanied you or not. If you wanted me to attend a wedding with you, a work happy hour, or a friend's party, I only agreed if it didn't conflict with my work schedule. Work was my priority. Why did I do that? I wanted to be with you. I got so sucked into the job that I couldn't see anything else. Tunnel vision. It was as though I was proving myself to my dad, my mom, to the world, and most of all to myself.

"I felt like such a fraud in the beginning. I got this big project and had no clue what I was doing. Instead of throwing in the towel, I worked ten times harder than everyone else and sacrificed my personal life and, yes, our relationship, and me. I lost those years to late nights and working weekends. And then I met Amy. By that time, I was feeling good at work. I had made it.

"And now I feel like that imposter again. I am in a role for which I am expected to be available twenty-four seven. And I hate it, hate that I have financial handcuffs that are squeezing me and the time I have with my family. I don't want to live like this. I don't want to see the disappointment and sadness in Amy's eyes anymore. I can't take it."

"You can do it differently this time. You know better; you do better. I always felt that you were bored with me in the end. You would fall asleep by nine o'clock, and I would see you for a whole thirty minutes, if that. I felt that I was never good enough or exciting enough to keep your attention. I thought we had a future and thought we were moving towards that. But in the end, it was as though I couldn't reach you, and in turn, I thought I was not good enough. There was something about me that wasn't lovable. We had invested three years, and in those last months, it was as if I didn't know you. You were physically present, but so mentally checked out and unavailable. I tried everything, did everything your way. I just felt so alone, but I stayed in it for the possibility of marriage.

"I totally lost myself, my voice. It was as though I never wanted to share my needs, and instead, I got angrier and angrier. I was ashamed of my needs. That's why I went on independent mode, never needing your help. Certainly never asking for it. You weren't there. Eventually, I shut down. And that's when we ended it, right on the stairs, just like the ones we are sitting on right now. Wow, that's irony."

As I shared my emotions, I connected to my hurt and desperation. At the time, I wanted it to work with Grayson so badly that I even stayed an extra year to hang in there. As time went by and our relationship stayed in limbo, my shame and rejection were overwhelming. Why would he not choose me? What was I missing? What did I lack? I couldn't take it physically, mentally, emotionally, or spiritually.

"Grace, I am so sorry. I never knew how much I hurt you. I was so focused on myself and my career that I had no clue about what you were going through or feeling. I grew up in a household where we did not talk about our feelings. When we were upset, we held it inside and stuffed it. Or we sucked it up and moved on. That was exactly what I did when you ended it. I threw my entire self into work. I didn't miss a beat. There could be no excuses nor distractions. Being successful was the only option. Period.

"The thing was, I really loved you the best way I could at the time. It was not about you. I blamed you for a lot of our issues, and I am so sorry. If I could take it back, I would, or at least do a better job of communicating my feelings. I am so grateful for you, our past, and now this encounter. This conversation has helped me see things that I wasn't in contact with before. I did not realize how checking out, not being present, nor physically or emotionally available really affects the people in my life. How destructive it is for the people I love.

"Grace, you have opened my eyes, and I will always be indebted to you. I need to go inside and save my marriage. I now know what to do, and it is because of you. Thank you." Grayson hugged me and said, "Goodbye, Grace."

And right there on the stairs, I finally received the acknowledgment I needed, and my own wounds—the ones from feeling I was never enough—started healing.

I understood the significance of being reunited with Grayson. I was loved and felt deep in my core that I mattered. It wasn't about Grayson giving me that. It was about my embracing my own love and support. Voicing my own feelings and sharing my emotions. I never did that in the physical world. I hate that, but never ever realized that I was staying busy in order to have a reason to disconnect from others. But now dead, I do feel more than when I was alive, and I am being compelled to confront my own emotions.

That's how we increase our capacity to love—we extend compassion and forgiveness to others. It starts with quieting the voice of judgment and increasing the kindness within ourselves.

I knew that this task was now complete. *I wonder what's on the horizon.*

♡

Exploration Questions
Chapter 6
Amy & Grayson

1. Grace was always late when she was alive. Do you show up on time, late, or early? Why do you think that is?

2. In what ways do you think relationships change after the kids come?

3. What patterns do you see in your relationships? Are you always dating the same type of person, meeting them in the same place, or doing the same type of activities?

4. Amy only moved once as a child and disliked being the "new girl." Did your family move around much? Was it difficult for you to be the "new kid"?

5. Grayson completely blows date night by letting work take priority. Has there been a time when you or your partner put work first and damaged your relationship?

Chapter 6 Activity

Plan a Date Night: If you are in a relationship, organize a date night for the two of you. Go to one of your favorite spots. If you are a singleton, take yourself out to a full dinner, not fast food. Get dressed up.

Chapter 7

Matthew

Here I am. Still in limbo. Am I trying to save my soul or heal it? Oh, who knows. Where's Enzo?

I see that I am back in my happy place, on a path located right next to the Central Park Reservoir. Enzo must be somewhere around here. This is our usual meeting spot. I am ready for him to come out from behind a tree, where he might be hiding. The sun is peeking through the clouds to remind me that the light is there. In due time, I guess I will walk toward it. Or can I jog or skip to it. It makes me think of the scene in *The Wizard of Oz* when Dorothy skips down the yellow-brick road. I enjoyed that story as a kid, although I could do without the creepy monkeys and that wicked witch. I don't want to think about that part of the movie. My past is all the scary I can handle. And even that is debatable at this point.

Speaking of daunting, here we go with the debrief. Enzo's back. "So what was it like to help out your ex and his wife? Kind of weird? No?"

"Wow, you just cut to the chase. No sugarcoating it, huh?"

"Now, don't you know me by now, Gracey? I'm a straight shooter. Why beat around the bush? I thought you would appreciate my direct approach."

I am annoyed by how much Enzo is enjoying this little banter. "Not sure about that," I mutter.

"Oh c'mon, lighten up. You completed the task with flying colors."

"Did I?"

"Absolutely. And for you, my dear…" From behind his back, he pulls out a white cup and saucer, an Americano for me.

It is a lovely surprise, and I am deeply touched by the gesture. "For a minute there, I forgot your smart-ass attitude." And then I smiled.

Receiving from others had never come easily for me. Maybe my walls were starting to come down a bit, and I was in contact with a depth that I hadn't had access to in a while. Deep down, I knew why Enzo was here, and it was not to give me my favorite earthly comfort, a cup of coffee. It was probably to chat about how my "learning journey" is going. I could see him pull out a clipboard with lots of questions, such as what worked well? what could you do differently? and what else would you like to share? I was used to this kind of work. At the end of a work project, I'd facilitate the postmortem process to determine and analyze successful or unsuccessful elements of the project.

As I expected, Enzo starts with a question, "Grace, let's get to it. So what did you learn? Sorry, this is part of the job that's not my favorite, but I do need to ask these questions. I could do without this official check-in. That is when I check in with the guy upstairs. I have to be on my best behavior, and you know that can be hard for me. I am always told that I am not as evolved as the other guides. Whateva that means."

Wow no room for chitchat here.

Enzo gets right to it. I prefer people who have a direct nature. You never have to figure out how they feel or where they stand. I appreciate that quality in people. That's how I rolled when I was alive. Except when it came to intimacy. I never wore my heart on my sleeve or trusted anyone enough to share what was really going on deep down. I always wore a mask that projected, "She's strong." I was all about powering through, and I believed that as time went on, I would eventually get over that need. When I began to feel weak, I avoided it at all costs. There were some things in life that I never resolved.

I can't even get to heaven because I am still cleaning up unfinished business.

I respond, "Let me think about this." I am still processing from each scenario. Both were significant males, and the relationships represented points in my life when I lost a piece of me. Each left me with negative beliefs and unresolved issues; you could call them wounds.

"Well, I guess I never got over the Jesse-and-Max event. After all those years, going back then and experiencing that as an adult, I reacted the same. I was paralyzed by fear during that experience. It took me right back to the pain of betrayal from Max and the intense fear of Jesse, his malicious nature. Their actions weren't the real tragedy. It was the story I created about myself, men, and the world. My innocence was lost, along with the ability to trust myself and others. If I look back again from where I am now, it was that I lost faith and trust in my decisions. I put myself in that abusive situation because I wanted to fit in and be part of the crowd. I really wanted Max to like me, and it was at my own cost."

Enzo asked, "Do you believe in forgiveness?"

"I guess, yes." Truthfully, I only answered that way because it was the right answer, not my real answer.

"You need to think about this more. Put more time in here. Maybe wait a bit to share your answer."

There was no fooling Enzo; he did not buy my response. We both dropped the question and moved on.

"I didn't realize that I still had all that baggage with Grayson. At first, I did not want to help him; I felt I had already wasted several years of my life on him. But when I spent time helping him, I remembered why I fell in love with him, and I was no longer resentful. I saw him hurting, and it was a turning point when he admitted that he needed help. He never would have said that when we were dating.

And that made me soften because I felt his vulnerability. I do think he is in a better place now to mend the brokenness of his marriage.

"I learned that some people in our lives are meant to be with us for seasons, but not for a lifetime. And that our worth can't be predicated on whether a relationship was cut short or even went the distance. I think that even when things end, we still have made an impact in that other person's life. And that was our journey. I was lucky. I had the opportunity to learn that I did make a difference in Grayson's life, even though I did not know it at the time.

"I guess the thing that makes me so sad is the way that Grayson looked at Amy. He never looked at me with that same level of love. I am not sure I ever received that look or had the feeling that I was loved unconditionally by a boyfriend."

"Love comes to us in different ways, Grace. Which brings you to your next adventure. Time and space are an illusion here. You will experience various moments in your life that will help provide you clarity and insights."

And here I am, in the front-passenger seat of a car, and it looks like we are heading to school. I am watching myself as a high school student. This is so weird. Oh yes, I remember this time. It's my senior year. I am with Matty. That's what I called him, not at first when we were freshmen, but once we became close friends as high school unfolded.

He lived about five minutes from me. Matt was an exceptional student; he excelled at mathematics and science, although he never boasted about his ease with those subjects. He was quiet about his intelligence. He was on the soccer team, which was quite a popular sport in a school that mostly prided itself on academics. He was six one and lean, although his coordination was less than desirable. His ticket into college would be his grades and SAT test scores. For most of our high school career, we were in different classes, except one. We did share the same English class. That was my best subject.

I had a way with words, writing essays. I had a love for books and started reading when I was four and found it hard to put a book down. I grew up reading books by Judy Blume and Laura Ingalls Wilder. One year, I got the *Little House on the Prairie* series under the Christmas tree, wrapped with a neat red-and-green-plaid bow. I was so excited that morning that I couldn't wait to start reading the first one. My love for the stories continued as I watched the series on TV. I adored Pa, Ma, Mary, and Laura. How could anyone not like Michael Landon? He was the best pa. He was epic on that show—always saved the day, always did the right thing.

My first encounter with Matthew was on the bus. He was plain rude. I had chosen the safe option of going to the middle of the bus to look for a seat. The front was for Goody Two-shoes, someone who always wanted to be the first to get to school. Heading towards the back was out of the question. The unwritten rule was that the older and coolest kids got those seats. It was challenging enough to be a freshman in high school; I needed to be smart as I embarked on that new adventure. Plus, it was a bit terrifying because I had no idea what to expect.

As I went to sit in the seat I had deemed safe, Matthew said, "Where are you going?" And he boxed me out by putting his butt down as quick as he could, so he could secure the seat.

The guy next to him laughed and said, "Matt, good move. We rule."

I was taken aback at first; then I quickly became annoyed. *Out of all the seats, he takes the one that I wanted. What a jerk?! Where is the male chivalry or politeness?* I gave him a look and under my breath said, "Whatever." Then I plunked down in the seat in front of him.

By the time I got into the school building and found my locker, the seat incident was in the back of my mind, but not forgotten. I always remembered the sting of that initial meeting. I still can't believe that we recovered and became such close friends by senior year.

By high school, I had already learned to avoid people who I felt were not really going to add value to my life. It made my circle somewhat on the smaller side, but at times I felt that open wound of being burned by people. My trust scale had to be super high to let anybody in. So instead of engaging with people, I dismissed them. Why should I spend any energy on them when I always had a good book at my fingertips that would transport me to another place and time—with more interesting people.

In my first three years of high school, I paid no attention to Matthew. I am now looking back and watching how our relationship shifted, how we got close. On the tennis court, that was the day it changed. *OMG, is that the tennis court?*

Here goes our story. Matty's and my friendship. It is fall semester of senior year; as the seasons changed, so did my relationship with Matthew. It all started with a tennis ball. I made the tennis team for three full consecutive seasons. I never identified with the athletic crowd. I hated it when people put labels on others. There were the geniuses, the athletes, the losers, and the favorites, although I never had the patience to keep up with all the names. People were more complex and deserved more than being put in a box or being stamped with a label.

About half past five, after hitting more than fifty serves across the net, which was my secret weapon, one of my balls went through a hole underneath the twelve-foot chain-link fencing that enclosed the tennis courts. *Oh great. So annoying.* I was always reaching under the wire to get the balls that escaped. As I would grab for them, there was a side to the fence where it stuck out; on several occasions, my tennis shorts almost got caught. *Ugh.* Normally, I would maneuver in a way that I missed getting hooked.

This time, no such luck, my shorts were stuck, and they were new. The last thing I wanted to do was move a certain way and rip them. I paid a pretty penny for them, which my mom was not on board with, but I appreciated their cut and style. When it came to my clothing, I didn't mind paying a bit more; it was an investment. However, my mom had already given me a lecture about how much I was spending on clothes, so I couldn't ruin these shorts.

I was stuck. *Oh crap, it's getting dark.* My teammates had left the courts about thirty minutes before, but I liked spending a little extra time perfecting my serve. *How can I get out of this mess and still salvage my shorts and dignity?* I look up and scan the area outside the courts, towards the soccer field, and there he is—Matthew.

He is a sweaty mess, covered in dirt from head to toe. Cleats, shin guards, and all. He stands with a smirk and a stare and then says, "Grace, need help?"

"Oh great," I say under my breath, then out loud, "What do you think?"

He responds, "I'll take that as a yes." He comes through the gate and onto the tennis court. He gently moves my body in a way that I get unhooked and without tearing my shorts.

I am relieved, yet at the same time feel humiliated. "Thanks."

"You're welcome."

Then I pack up my racket and leave as fast as I can. *Now I owe him for my dignity and intact tennis shorts.*

I was out the gate, heading toward the girls' locker room, when I heard him say, "You're welcome."

The next day, I am grabbing my algebra textbook and running late to my first-period math class, which was typical behavior. It was so hard to get out of bed; sleep was something that I really needed daily. I honored the eight-hour sleep rule.

Matt appears. "Hey, Grace, what's up? Get home okay yesterday?"

I am a bit taken aback by his pleasantries; during the first two years of high school, our paths barely crossed. Which was fine by me. I never was impressed with him and had felt that way since our first meeting on the bus.

"Yeah, I did. Hey, thanks again for helping me out."

He chuckled briefly until he saw the look on my face. "You were in a tough spot," he said.

"Go ahead. Get all your jokes out, so we don't have to bring this up again."

He was quick to change the subject. "Hey, you want to get a slice at Gino's by our house? I go there sometimes after school."

"Don't you have soccer practice?"

"It's a short one. The coach has some personal commitment, so he's leaving early. Why, do you have tennis?"

I kind of was hoping that I could use practice as an excuse. My first instinct was to change the subject. "Not officially, but I do like to get in fifty serves…keep my game up."

Matt asked, "How long does that take?"

"About an hour."

"Okay, I'll be done by three thirty, and we can head there together. I have my car. Meet in the parking lot by three forty-five. You okay with that?"

I wasn't sure if I even wanted to go, but now I felt bad about backing out. He had helped me yesterday, so I replied, "Yeah, okay."

Later that afternoon, I glanced down at my watch to see it was three fifty-five. "Oh crap, I'm late." I sprint to the parking lot, my tennis racket not fully in its case and my book bag dangling over my shoulder, and arrive a good ten minutes late. *What a hot mess I am!*

Matt said, "I wasn't sure if you were coming, but you made it."

I am a bit winded. "Yeah, I am here. Lost track of time."

Matt opens the car door and says, "Let's go. I'm starving."

I am happy that, within twenty minutes, we get to the pizza parlor and head to the nearest table to order. I am not shy when it comes to eating, and at this moment my hunger has kicked into high gear.

Starving is a more appropriate word, and the wafting smell of bread, cheese, and tomato sauce is making me hungrier.

Matt goes to the counter and orders a large pepperoni pie and breadsticks. I am thankful that there will be an ample amount of food. He even throws in a Caesar salad, but I am more interested in the good stuff. *Bring on the pizza.*

After ten minutes of focused eating, Matt starts the conversation. "So you think that you will play tennis in college?"

Kind of a random question since I never really considered myself an athlete. Playing sports in college was a full-time job, and everyone had to be crazy good, even to get into a Division III school. I never had that kind of passion for tennis or any other sport. I dabbled a little in volleyball and soccer, but never had either the skill or interest to invest the time. When I was in eighth grade, I decided to only focus my efforts on tennis. I loved playing singles; it was my opponent, racket, ball, net, and I. No other distractions.

"No. I don't have either the skills or the desire. I like it for high school or playing in the summer at my pool club, but that's all."

At that moment, I pictured myself as an adult, being married, heading to the club with a stroller, and dropping my kid off so I could hit a few balls with other moms. That was a vision that seemed extremely far away.

"How about you? Planning on playing soccer at college?"

He laughed and nearly choked while taking a sip of his Coke. "Nah, my strengths are with the books. Using my mind is easier than using my body. My height compensates for my lack of coordination on the field."

I ask, "So what is important to you in life? What are you all about?"

Matt is taken aback by my directness, yet at the same time appreciates it. "Wow, okay. Let me think about it. I am more of a science and math guy. Nothing real exciting, although I am fascinated with astronomy. The study of space—planets, stars, and not really the other unearthly phenomena. And numbers don't lie. They are very straightforward. It is about solving a puzzle. The pieces always come together; you need to be patient and look at all the angles. People, on the other hand, are not so easy, are overly complex. Let's take US history; the US presidents are all so different, and in order to understand their motives, you need to look deep into their psyche and go behind their curtains. That's why I stick to numbers; there's a truthfulness when they tell their story."

Once I had some food in my stomach, I became more present and interested in the conversation. *Does the boy that stole my seat freshman year have a bit of depth?*

I said, "My favorite subject is English. I love the written word and am obsessed with reading a book from start to finish in one sitting. I enjoy stepping into a world and experiencing it from the characters' perspectives. It is a good escape. The writer's word choice and how the story unfolds is fascinating for me. I also like learning other languages."

We sit there for another two hours, bonding over how we are already OVER high school and ready for a new adventure. Which is soon, since we are in the fall year as seniors. This conversation was the real start of our friendship.

I graduated to calling him Matty, as opposed to Matthew or Matt, which other people used. He would on occasion call me Gracey. Months would go by when we would go for a slice on every Wednesday, but I always made sure that there were some greens involved in our afternoon snack. I liked color in my diet. It was something that I learned about from one of my mom's friends.

Matthew's parents gave him a car as a bribe to make sure that he could easily get to and from the library. They were counting on his getting an academic scholarship; otherwise, he would have to stay and study at a local school. That was not what he wanted, so there was an element of pressure he felt, more than his friends experienced. He never complained and kept quite cool about it, at least externally.

We rode together to and from school. We were in the same English class, and our weekly pizza runs helped us develop a strong friendship. Well, that is what I thought; I could be myself with him and felt safe with him. I hope he felt the same. I didn't have to put on any pretenses or put on a fake front because I wanted him to like me.

Although I did not realize it at the time, Matty had a real gift of giving me my space to be myself, no matter what was going on with me or how I looked. He never judged, and he appreciated my quirkiness.

The Senior Dance was coming up in April, not the typical prom timing. Most schools' big dances would be in May or June. Our dance was called Spring Fling and was held in early April, as a tribute to a new season and a celebration for the last couple of months of high school. It was different than the official prom because no one was required to bring a date. Students picked a group of people and shared a table with them. You could have all-girls or all-boys tables. Generally, there was some mix of sexes, but the ratios varied. I preferred this approach since I did not like feeling the pressure of bringing a date, coordinating colors in attire, or even having to buy a boutonniere. I never was into events that had a lot of pomp and circumstance. I thought that I may regret not going one day, so I knew that I should go. It would be the talk of the town, and all my friends would be discussing it prior to the day, on the day, and during the rest of the year.

I found myself being the organizer of the table. In some ways, it was just easier for me to take charge. I liked being in control. I did not always trust my friends to make it happen and follow through on getting the task completed. Some may define me as a control freak, whereas I saw it as a way to guarantee that everything would happen.

It was ten to a table, and interestingly enough, our table was an even mix, five girls and five boys; there was one official couple, Amanda and Jonathan. They had started dating back at the beginning of junior year. Everyone else was just friends who got along well.

Thank God, there was no real drama in the bunch. I lacked patience when it came to fuss and commotion; people should just get along. What was there really to fight about? We were in high school, not solving real-world problems. Of course, Matty was going to the dance; he was the easiest to work with in the bunch.

I was in charge of picking up the tickets, coordinating the transportation to and from the dance, and using my house as a beginning spot where we would take some photos. Parents could or could not come, whichever they wanted, and the kids would leave together from one location to head to the dance.

The night of the Spring Fling was here. I had to admit all the plans were falling into place. It pleasantly surprised me; usually something goes wrong at these things. My parents were thrilled to have everyone in their front yard. My mom always felt that our front porch would come in handy someday. She had her wicker chairs with plaid pillows and small tables scattered around if somebody wanted to put their lemonade down as they were reading a book. Generally, it was I who was sitting out there most summer days with a good read.

The ten young adults arrived with their families, all presenting in different attires. Two were more casual, wearing jeans and a sports coat, while a couple of the others were wearing black tuxes, and then everything in between. Most of the girls—except for my best friend, Hope, and me—were wearing ankle-length gowns. Hope and I always had our own style; we went for short dresses, above the knee. I was in standard black, and Hope went with a Burgundy-wine color. Matty was dressed in between with a navy sports coat, blue shirt, khaki pants, and a red- and navy-striped tie. That was his version of sophistication since he wasn't much into designers or getting all dolled up. He was more about jeans, golf shirts, and sweaters. More of a classic look, not about trendy. My look was trendier or had an edge.

I never liked to admit it, but when I picked up a piece of clothing, I was drawn in by its name brand. The designer brands fit better and had a more creative look. I did not want to be known for that because, secretly, I felt a bit disgusted by my extravagant taste.

Photos were taken, the adults drank wine, and we all headed into the limo to our Senior Spring Fling. We were on time, en route, and joyful to get our dancing shoes on and drink some punch. I wondered if I would taste anything else, maybe someone added a bit more ingredient to the concoction. It didn't seem that anyone had that idea or had the guts to add alcohol.

As we headed to the dance, I noticed a change in Matty. He was usually a bit on the introverted side, but that night he was unusually quiet as we sat next to each other in the limo. The group all piled out of the vehicle and headed into the school gym. It was decorated with Mylar helium balloons in colors of silver and white. On each table, there were a couple of small bouquets in a vase with a pale-green ribbon wrapped around it—the school's lame attempt to represent spring. In any event, I didn't care; I was more intrigued by what people were wearing, as opposed to the spring-themed aesthetics.

The DJ played a slow song. There was Matty with a serious look on his face. He seemed so stoic. "Grace, would you like to dance?" I was surprised by how official and serious he was about the question.

"Sure." In that moment the vibe between us changed; I felt it instantly.

Matty in a shaky voice and a stomach full of nerves said, "Grace, you are my best friend. And I know that our first meeting on the bus was not a good one. My feelings have changed in the last year. Riding to school, English class, after-school pizza runs…well, I have fallen for you. I like all your quirks and idiosyncrasies. You're smart, beautiful, and you're special. Grace, I love you."

I was silent and speechless. My heart was pounding a mile a minute. I felt suffocated, like a twenty-pound weight had been placed on my chest. I couldn't move; I was paralyzed and didn't know what to say or do to get out of the situation. There was only one other time that I could remember feeling that way—such intensity, all eyes on me—in the playground.

Most girls would be thrilled to hear a boy say something like that. Here's my best friend, opening his heart and acknowledging how extraordinary I am. I should have been elated and on cloud nine, but instead, I felt sick. It terrified me. My first instinct was to run for the hills—not a slow jog, but a sprint—but there was no way I could do that to Matty.

He knew—by the look on my face and my dead silence that seemed to last an hour—that I did not feel the same way. I stopped dancing, which confirmed what Matty knew in his gut. He was a guy dedicated to science, who always needed proof, real data, but he'd stalled on the dance floor. It was his stomach that told him the truth.

I couldn't make eye contact. My eyes focused on the floor, and I felt shame.

Matty had to say something. The atmosphere was so uncomfortable that he was jumping out of his skin. "You don't feel the same way." The way he said it was more of a statement than a question.

I couldn't even give him the courtesy of looking at him. I felt horrible because it was true. In ways, his heart was so much more open than mine, and he had a bigger capacity to love. I didn't know why, but I didn't feel the same way. Even though I felt safe with him and could be myself, I could not surrender to his love and truly be open to receive it. Matty was the last person on the entire planet whom I wanted to cause any pain or hurt. What I didn't want to happen, just did, and I couldn't do anything to take it back or even make it better. He knew, and I knew—our relationship changed once Matty said the words "I love you."

I nodded. "Matty, I am so sorry."

After I finished my sentence, Matty left the dance floor and walked out the gym doors. I didn't see him the rest of the dance, and barely during the summer months prior to heading to college. It saddened me, but out of respect, I kept my distance; plus, I never really knew the best way to handle this situation.

All of a sudden, it's Big Grace; I'm an adult, back on the scene and seeing this situation so differently. For the first time since I died, I feel more human. *How does this happen?* I can feel my feet touch the ground as I walk. I am in human form for this moment, but a strong energy is taking me to the wing where I remember all the science classes were. It wasn't an area of high school that I frequented much because I was drawn to English, and even foreign-language subjects. I am now walking down my old high school hallway, which is flooded with blue lockers. I pass my old locker, number 373. *Why can I remember that?* I haven't thought about this place for years, let alone thought about my locker number. *So weird. Why am I being drawn to this time as a high school student?* The smell, the decorations, and the music are bringing back those same feelings from my senior year.

Actually, they are much stronger now. This is so strange because I am a grown adult, actually a dead adult, and this happened over twenty years ago. Now I see how this moment imprinted my soul.

There he is, sitting on the floor right next to the physics room. Oh yeah, I remember now; this was his favorite place to hang. Even though so many years have gone by, it is as if we never went our separate ways. Truthfully, I am excited to see him.

As I get closer, I feel a tidal wave of sadness come over me. I feel the depth of his hurt and pain. And the worst part about it—I caused this. It was because of me. Matty loved me, and I broke his heart. I see his knees close to his chest and his head down, and I finally realize where he had disappeared to that night. I never saw him again that night because this is where he was, licking his wounds.

As I move closer, Matty's head comes up, and he looks at me. His eyes are red and a little puffy, like he's been crying. Suddenly his expression changes into something less sad and more confused.

"Who are you? You look familiar."

Of course, I do. I just broke your heart fifteen minutes ago. I rack my brain to come up with a believable answer.

The best I can do is "I am friends with Mr. Stevens and helping him with the Spring Fling. A chaperone."

I was not sure he would buy it. It helped that he was so distracted and consumed with emotions. Otherwise, I knew he was much too curious and would be asking more questions. Although I already knew, I still asked the pressing question, "What's wrong?"

I see Matty pause, not one to share his feelings or wear his heart on his sleeve. The only person he would do that with just broke his heart, so he may not say anything in this moment, especially not talk about his current emotional state.

But Matty surprised me; he was so vulnerable and open. Maybe secretly he knew who I really was. But how would he?

"Well, not sure why I am telling you this, but for some reason I feel that I can trust you. Kind of weird. You seem familiar. I just got rejected by my best friend. I just told her I love her, and she doesn't feel the same way. So that is that. I should have kept my mouth shut and not said anything."

In that moment, I came from an energy of compassion and love. I wanted to do better. Make it right. I couldn't change what happened, but maybe I could be there for Matty now.

"Well, I guess you could have kept quiet, but what would that have accomplished? You would have always wondered if she felt the same way."

Matty sighs. "I guess. But now I just feel like such shit and so stupid."

As the curse word came out of his mouth, I saw him pause. He was probably questioning if that was such a good idea, saying it in front of an adult. Although, I was not too bothered by it, so I thought it must have been only a fleeting thought for Matty.

"Look, you have your whole life ahead of you. And I know you feel like shit right now, but know that there will be other girls, women.

And maybe this girl just couldn't open her heart to you. For some reason or another, she didn't have the capacity to really be fully available to the gift you were offering her."

He gives me a confusing look, so I do my best to explain. "What I mean is that maybe she was not ready for true love, or just couldn't be vulnerable right now. It takes a lot of courage to do what you did. You put your heart on the line, and that takes guts. Sometimes people are not ready for that. It doesn't make them bad or mean or uncaring; they're just not ready. Or maybe she was not really a part of your life plan. I am starting to learn that people come into our lives for a reason. Maybe some are meant to be with you for many years, but others for just a season. Do you understand?"

Matty looked lighter and nodded his head in agreement. He understood and remembered other girls he'd liked, but that hadn't worked out. I'm sure he's fine now, even though it seemed at the time that he would never get over his heartbreak and disappointment.

Then Matty said, "So what now?"

"You get up, go back in there, feel good that you were brave, and know you will be okay. More than okay. Any girl would be lucky to have you. It is all about timing." I said it with conviction because, in that moment, I knew his future. Matty will grow up and have a family. One beautiful wife, one dog, and two sons who will be part of his journey.

I start walking away, knowing that deep in his spirit, Matty got it. He understood.

Matty calls out from a distance, "Hey!" I am about to turn the corner when I hear, "What's your name?"

I make sure I reply loud enough so that he can hear me, "It's Grace," and I continue moving forward because that is where the energy is guiding me.

As I leave, I am reminded of all the good times in high school with my bestie, Hope, and how much I truly miss her.

♡

Exploration Questions
Chapter 7
Matthew

1. Central Park is Grace's happy place. Where is yours?

2. Grace says, "I never wore my heart on my sleeve or trusted anyone enough to share what was really going on deep down." When have you worn your heart on your sleeve?

3. In which ways can you expand your circle to make sure more champions are in your life?

4. How have your friendships evolved throughout your life?

5. Grace broke Matty's heart on the dance floor. When have you had to tell someone that you didn't feel the same way they did? How did you handle it?

Chapter 7 Activity

Reconnect with Classmates: Get out your high school yearbook. It's time to reminisce. Are you still in contact with any of your classmates? Which ones would it be fun to see again?

Chapter 8

Nonno Joseph

After seeing Matty and me in that slow-dance moment, I'm left with such a huge pit in my stomach. I can't shake it; it is a heavy weight, an immense amount of disappointment and failure. For the first time, I am contemplating the thought that maybe I am the problem. Maybe the real deal was that I was unable to receive the love that came my way. I never thought about it this way. I always thought that I was just poor at picking men and was a magnet for any unavailable men, that I was attracted to the ones who fell into that camp. For me, there is some truth to that; maybe being unavailable and unattainable was safe for me.

Now I am second-guessing myself because Matty was someone with a huge heart, and he was open to loving me in the ways I deserved. But I rejected him; I ran from him. In so many words, I said, "No thanks." I see now I was not ready or open to it. I couldn't receive his love.

Now my brain is swirling. Was that the case with all the men in my life? Did I miss out by rejecting love that came my way?

Isn't it time for the debrief with Enzo? Oh, he will have a field day with this one. Where is he?

As I am unraveling, my energy turns to regret, as opposed to curiosity. Then I remember a safe place in my life. A place where I went when I felt out of sorts. A place where I went to just sit with my emotions, mainly the sad and angry ones. As my thoughts connect to my safe place, I literally am transported there.

Oh my God. I am here. Wow, moving through time and space is such a trip. Literally.

I am on my grandpop's, Nonno's, front porch. Joseph was Nonno's name. I'd call him Nonno. He lived about twenty minutes from my house. It was a multifamily, three-story home. I think my grandparents thought that when their kids got older, they would occupy one story of the house with their families. It never worked out that way. However, they would continuously host other family members from Italy when they came to this country for the first time. At that point in time, it was all about creating a better life for their families. The American dream.

When I was little, we would go to Nonno's for Sunday dinner. It would always be the same menu: some meats and cheeses with a bowl of olives for an appetizer, followed by a huge tray of lasagna, along with extra gravy—other people call it marinara sauce—and meatballs and sausage, stuffed artichokes, salad with vinegar and oil, and tons of bread from the local bakery.

One summer, I decided to give up meat, and that did not go over well with the family. I gave that a couple of months and found myself craving a meatball. By September, I caved in and added the meatball to my plate. My vegetarian stage was for a hot minute.

For me, I was always waiting for what was on the table for dessert. My personal favorite was the cannoli with fluffy, sweet ricotta and chocolate chips. Although, they would change it up from time to time; sometimes they would have the Italian rainbow cookies, biscotti, tiramisu, and even a cheesecake once in a while.

We would have to be there by 3:00 p.m.; if not, Nonna, my grandmother, would say, "Where you been? The food is getting cold."

I think that is where my love of food came from, although as I got older, I expanded my palate and deeply enjoyed other cuisines, like French food. Truth be told, my first love for bread and cheese came from my Italian upbringing.

Back to the porch—it is white and wraps around the entire house. There's an American flag hanging right by the door. This brings me back to the time when my grandfather built that porch. It was a labor of love and took him two months to finish; as a kid, it felt like an eternity. It was the same as when we were getting close to Christmas. December always dragged along; to me, it seemed like the longest month. I am sure it bugged my parents when I asked every two seconds, "When is Santa coming? Is he here yet?"

I remember Nonno saying that I could be the very first one to sit on the porch with him. And as far as I know, he made good on that promise. I always sat right next to him. I'd have first dibs on the rocking chair, and I sipped from my favorite mug as I rocked. It was a mug that displayed Strawberry Shortcake and her friends. I loved Blueberry Muffin. I had the doll, and then my grandparents bought me the mug. I would have all my drinks in that thing, up until high school. *Come to think of it, whatever happened to that mug?*

Suddenly, a familiar man, whom I adored and loved, appeared before me, holding my favorite mug in his hand.

"Nonno, what are you doing here? Oh my God, there's my mug."

My eyes fill with happiness as I see one of the men who adored me from my first day on this planet. And that mug, it reminds me of the comforts of home. *What's in it? Can I drink it?*

"Hi, Gracey, so good to see you, sweetheart."

Besides Matty, he was the only one whom I allowed to call me that nickname.

"You are the apple of my eye. I've been watching over you. You were such a hard worker. You take after me, you know. I've been working since I was eleven. I knew I had to work hard to create a good life for my family. Plus, I can't sit still. It always annoyed Nonna." He chuckled. Then with a loving glance, he said, "Gracey, you are beautiful. *Bellissima!*"

He really sees me…but then, he always could. He has a special place in my heart. I remembered our outings, just Nonno and I in the car, traveling to our next location. Church on Sunday mornings, eating an ice-cream cone at Carvel, or even walking around the park for some fresh air. I enjoyed being with him.

In ways, he softened me up; he was so sensitive and emotional. His eyes filled up every time there was a sentimental commercial on the television, when we were leaving to go home, and every time they had a family photo, capturing the holiday filled with delicious food, wine, and love. He always wore his heart on his sleeve, although his sensitivity was more apparent as he got older and when he was diagnosed with cancer.

That time was difficult for me and tugged at my heartstrings. Sadness was my least favorite emotion with which to connect. I avoided it, and going numb was my go-to in order to escape. When I saw how emotional Nonno was, I knew he was dying. I couldn't admit that I would be losing one of my biggest champions. Avoidance was a way to deny the potential loss of Nonno. Although, in August of 1992, that day came, and from then on, I had a hole in my heart, especially during big holidays, like Thanksgiving and Christmas.

Now, Nonno was here with me, and that was definitely one of the perks of my being dead—or, shall I say, in limbo.

Again, I ask, "What are you doing here? I am so happy that you are here and that you found me. I've missed you all of these years."

"Gracey, I am with you. Always. I was there when you graduated college, moved into your first apartment in Boston, and accepted your first job offer as a marketing coordinator. I was even with you on your last day on Earth. I—my soul, that is—never left you.

"I even came to visit you. Remember that dream that you had right after I died? We were driving in the car, and I looked at you and smiled. You felt my love, even when you woke up. That was my way of saying, 'You are not alone, Grace.' I am here for you always, sweetheart. Even if you don't see me in the flesh, I am here in spirit.

Our bond and connection are strong; nothing will stand in the way of it. I have loved you from the day you were born, and that will last forever."

I tear up. In that moment, I deeply feel every ounce of his love and support. No walls and barriers, just openness and the flow of his spirit. *Wow, I'm getting good at this feeling stuff.*

As tears are streaming down my face, I ask, even though I am hesitant to hear the answer, "Was I so closed off from love?"

There was such a part of me that could not receive love, especially from the boys and men in my life. Deep down, I was terrified of rejection. So I either closed myself off or went for emotionally unavailable men. I did not even realize this about myself. I always thought that I wasn't lovable or that I was unlucky in love. I can see now that there was a part of me that I held back and that was unavailable to the men in my life. It was not about them. I can see now that I couldn't trust myself.

"Gracey, I feel that you are doubting yourself. Beating yourself up is no good. Don't do that."

I said, "I see now I made bad choices and lost myself in most of my relationships. It was more about what my boyfriend wanted, as opposed to respecting my limits and my needs. I never wanted to show a lot of vulnerability. Maybe I felt that they wouldn't stick around if they knew about my real needs and desires. I decided to play it safe and stuff my feelings and needs within me. I never expressed them. I preferred to walk away, rather than really share who I was. Now I realize that the only person that got to see me was Matty; he knew."

"He's not the only one." Nonno smiled.

"Okay, you're right, Nonno. I now see that Matty knew me more than I knew myself. He accepted and loved me for all that I was. At the time, I just didn't see it. There was a part of me that did not see my true value. What I feel so sad about is that I never learned that lesson when I was alive, and now it is too late. How did I miss this? And don't say something to make me feel better. Tell the truth, Nonno. Please."

My grandpop always had that tenderness and soft side. He helped me connect with my vulnerability. He was a safe space for me when I skinned my knee or fought with my sibling. He was always a calming source for me.

"Gracey, it's never too late. Soon, you'll be movin' on to your next journey. The learning is there and right in front of you. You have to do the work. You can do this! And you gotta give yourself a break. As a kid, you were so hard on yourself. So tough. Can you be more compassionate with yourself?"

I think about what he's saying. Even as a little girl, there was always a part of me that I wished were more carefree, that would dance in circles and be silly. Reading my books was a way to escape, be in my mind, and avoid interacting with the world. I loved that I could step into other worlds by opening a book. It was safe and easy for me. *Was that bad?*

"Gracey, it's not about being right or wrong, *or* good and bad. What did you learn from your life? Honey, your heart is so big and full of love. I think at times it was difficult for you to show it. And maybe this entire task is supposed to teach you to love *you*! I am here to remind you that, no matter what you've done or what mistakes you've made, you are so lovable. It is not about what you do; it is who you are. Like Matty, I have always seen you."

"Was I a good granddaughter?"

"The best. Honey, it is not about good or bad. I always felt your love and knew how lovable you were, even when you were fighting with your sister and brother. You knew just what to say and what to do to provoke them." He said that last line with a smile.

I beamed and said, "I want to make sure that you know how important you are to me and how much I love you. You died so quickly, and I never got to say that to you. It is one of my biggest regrets."

"Oh Gracey, I always knew, my love. I always knew."

Tears of relief are running down my eyes as I release that remorse. I'd held on to it ever since the grandfather I loved died before I got to say goodbye. It was such a relief that I could now let that go. Nonno always had such good timing. He would call me and say hi when I needed him most, or take me to Carvel and buy me an ice cream when I needed a lift. And now he was doing it again, just by being here in this moment.

"Gracey, I have to go. I already broke the rules by staying here longer than I was supposed to. As you are focused on your own path, I need to get back to mine. I have plenty to work through." He laughed. "Gotta go, Gracey."

I reached for him and hugged him. I went for it; I did not care if it was "legal." I mean, I was dead, and so was my grandpop, but the same energy and spirit were there. I could feel the warmth of his soul, and that topped off the healing. I felt complete and thought it was closure for him as well. Deep down in my soul, I now had peace because I know I will see my favorite person again, so the sadness went away. In my heart, I'll connect with him again, although I am not sure when exactly. But I guess that is all part of the process—trust in the timing and have faith in myself. That is all part of the learning, my learning.

Man, this stuff is not easy.

I think I am starting to have a bit more patience. You know who had patience in my life? Hope. She came to my mind earlier. I do miss her. Come to think of it, she got me as well. I was a very loyal friend to her, maybe not as closed as I with others. *I wonder how she is doing?*

♡

Exploration Questions
Chapter 8

Nonno Joseph

1. Have your grandparents been a big part of your life? Did or do they live nearby?

2. What is your favorite memory of spending time with your grandparents?

3. How was your relationship with your grandparents different than the one with your parents?

4. Are there other family members who have supported you? Listened to your secrets and concerns?

5. What type of family traditions have you carried on?

Chapter 8 Activity

Assemble a Family-Recipe Collection: Do you have old index cards with family recipes? An old cookbook with handwritten notes? Gather them up, and photocopy them to create a collection you can share with other family members. Old recipes can be photocopied and framed for sentimental family gifts.

Chapter 9

Hope

I was still basking in the light of Nonno when Enzo appeared. "Helllooo, Grace, how are you doing?"

"I am at peace. Very content. Nonno stopped to visit. He is still one of my favorite people in the universe." The planet was not big enough for the love I had for him. "His soul is alive. I feel so incredibly grateful to have been able to see and experience his love again. Thank you."

"Can't take credit for Joe, Joseph, or as you call him, Nonno. It was from the guy upstairs. It was his doing." Enzo pointed straight up to the sky.

"Aren't we already upstairs?"

Enzo belted out a big belly laugh. "Not yet. You'll know when you're officially upstairs. Good news. You are moving in the right direction."

I am so torn. I am still drawn to the simple earthly pleasures, like a slice of pizza, a hot Americano, and a good book. *What will it be like once I leave Earth for good? Will my favorite things be there?*

Enzo requests, "I need a favor from you. This person really needs your help. She is so discouraged when it comes to love. You are the best person for the job, or I guess I better say the right spirit to handle this situation."

I was about to go into question mode; that was my superpower. I'm great at asking all sorts of questions. At performance-feedback sessions, my managers always told me I was inquisitive. I asked questions to get clients thinking. Meetings lasted a bit longer because, in the end, I always asked a question that others had not thought of. The analytical types—STs, Sensing and Thinking from the Myers-Briggs personality test—always appreciated my attention to detail. The visionaries, big-picture types, wanted to jump out the window when it came to answering all my never-ending questions. When it came to my personal life, my detailed nature drove others crazy, but I needed all the data before making a decision. It was a blessing and a curse.

As I was about to ask my first question, Enzo disappeared once again. *Ugh, I hate when he does that.* I am not sure why I still get worked up and surprised by it. Enzo does this all of the time. All that was left was an essence of his spirit.

As I was stewing, suddenly I am transported to a new place, and this time I recognize it right away. That couch I was very familiar with. It was a second home and a safe space to be. It was Hope's apartment.

Hope has been my best friend since the eighth grade. She is my opposite, a bit on the flighty side, and goes for things on a whim if they feel right to her. When Hope goes against her intuition, she pays the price. The decision inevitably leads to disaster, and then she beats herself up for days for not listening to her inner voice. She is a perpetual optimist and always sees the best in people. I always made fun of that trait and teased her about it. But I secretly admired her for the faith she had in people and her ability to throw caution to the wind. She was all about going for things, even without all the data.

I am in such a whirlwind with this journey that I never got a moment to miss my BFF. Hope was my person; I never judged her for the decisions that she made, especially when it came to men. She had my back, even when I knew deep down giving the relationship another try was a mistake. Hope never judged me. That is the true gift of friendship.

I wish Hope could see me, and we could stay up all night drinking at least one bottle of red wine. Maybe we could be adventurous and finish off two bottles…with a veggie pizza. The fact that we always ordered veggies on our pizza made us both feel less guilty the next morning, despite the hangover.

There's Hope in a baggy cotton hoodie with gray leggings, standing in front of her makeshift closet, which is located right by the bathroom. I can tell she is perplexed about what to wear. Her closet is a bunch of wood planks that were built to hold towels and toiletries. She lives in Chelsea, which is on the West Side of Manhattan; when it comes to property in the city, closet space is a luxury.

That did not stop Hope; she found a way to make space for her stuff. Not that she needed a lot of stuff. She is definitely more of a minimalist. Hope is creative; she was able to transform a nook of shelves into an extension of the small closet she had in the corner of the room. She was always proud of the ways she would be innovative and efficient with the space.

Back when I joined Hope on her apartment search and the realtor described the unit as cozy, I had to do my best to have a poker face and not show my real feelings. The reality is the place was tiny, and the realtor was saying anything, just so she could rent it out. Hope knew it was small, but when she walked through the door, it felt like home to her. And frankly, it was all that she could afford at the time. Ten years later, she still resides in the apartment. Not because of budgetary reasons, but because she enjoys her little piece of happiness in a twelve-story building. Hope was never much into stuff or high-end furnishings; it was all about the neighborhood feel and those who surrounded her.

Hope loves Anna, who lives next door and invites Hope over for tea and pastries on Sundays; Anna tells Hope stories about her family in Italy and about moving to this country. Anna's family was from Milan, and she emigrated to this country for the love of a man. Also, America was all about possibilities—freedom, options, and space wrapped up in a neat bow. Anna reminds Hope of her grandmother, and she always appreciates Anna's invitations to share confections and conversations.

In Manhattan, your neighbors, friends, and the community become your family. During times of crisis, like September 11, Hope found the city always bonded together—New York Strong! Hope felt that New Yorkers got a bum rap. She found them to be kind and generous, especially in times of crisis and change.

I can see that Hope isn't acting like her old self. I'd been so wrapped up in my own thing that I hadn't thought about the impact of my death on Hope. I know if the tables were turned, I would be devastated. I feel her heavy heart and the sadness. It is palpable and permeates her body, especially around her heart and in her eyes. I was told once that the eyes are the windows of the soul. As I sense Hope's emptiness, I know it is due to losing me. I was her soul sister, her bestie. And her heart, I know it's broken, and if I were in her shoes, I would not know how to recover, even with all her self-care practices—meditation, daily affirmations, writing in her journal, and even a good cry when it's needed. There is so much loss coming from Hope that it breaks my heart to see how sad she is. It is intense, and I can feel the void inside her that she cannot fill. Not now, maybe not ever.

I was the person whom Hope consulted every time she went on a date. I always knew that right outfit and look, depending on the timing, location, and activity planned for the date. It's one of my gifts. Hope picked out options, but they were never quite right. Somehow, I always found a better choice. Now she had to do it all alone. And she no longer had anyone with whom she could really debrief her dates. I was her person, but now I was gone. She must feel abandoned. There is no one who can replace our twenty-plus years of friendship. Hope's heart and soul knows it undeniably and fully feels the loss. And now I have a moment to feel it as well.

Wow, this is rough. So what am I doing here?

And right on cue, there he is. "Enzo, nice of you to join the party. Now are you going to explain why I am here. I get it, she is devastated, and now I am feeling an immense amount of sadness. It is overwhelming."

"Your friend is struggling here. You did leave her. Disappeared suddenly. She does not even want to go on this date. She was not like this when you were on Earth. At times, you both were a bit cynical, and trusting people was not your strength. But you gotta admit, Hope is optimistic, looks at challenges as learning opportunities. She used to be a 'glass full' kind of girl, but now she is in a funk, buried in a black cloud. Can you believe that she doesn't wanna go on this date? This is not like her; you gotta fix this."

He was right. Hope was always game to meet a new man and see what happened. She never wanted the traditional route of marriage and kids, but always longed for a soul mate, someone she could fully be herself with and connect with on a spiritual level. I can feel that she has lost a piece of her heart.

Enzo continues, "But now with the loss of her beloved Gracey— yes, *you*—she is giving up on love and doesn't see all the good in the world. She is feeling both defeated and angry. Her emotions fluctuate by the hour, and she really doesn't know how to manage these mood swings. This is not her soul's path; to be alone is not her destiny. You need to do something about this. Got it? Capisci? This is her first date since your memorial. And all I can say is, this is an important event. Don't let her blow it."

"Wow, no pressure here, Enzo."

Hope never loved getting all dolled up for the occasion; that was more my thing. I loved getting ready for dates, choosing colors, jewels, and of course some kick-ass shoes. Hope was more Bohemian; the natural look was more her thing. Something that flowed, nothing real tight. She loved patterns and comfy fabrics, and those reflected her personality. Free People and Anthropologie were her favorite stores to browse and find new wardrobe options. Only sale items were fair game.

Only once did Hope venture into a formfitting, elegant gown. It was for a black-tie wedding at the Plaza Hotel in Manhattan. She told me she was uncomfortable and could not breathe the entire night. But she admitted that in that dress, she'd attracted more men's eyes than usual.

At the time, I said, "See, I told you. Show off the bod. You do have a gorgeous figure!"

Hope blushed and said, "Okay, maybe I'll wear it another time." But that never happened. She kept it in her closet for another year and then donated it to Goodwill. "It is a beautiful dress. Let someone else enjoy it so that it won't go to waste."

Unfortunately, for this upcoming date, she can't call me to strategize on the outfit, or even share the details of the guy she's going out with. Truthfully, I can sense that she does not even want to go. Being in her presence, I can feel that she is down on love. And it goes even deeper. Hope is down on life. Like she has to talk herself into it.

I hear Hope talking to herself and rambling, "I know the polite thing to do is to go. I already cancelled once. I know it is my work friend's brother. Brittney is nice enough, so I am sure her brother is as well. She really has been pushing this blind date for the past six months, bringing up her brother's name at least once a week when I bump into her. Although she did stop mentioning it for two months after I lost Grace. That was helpful. I just really have not been up to going out. My heart is not in it. I usually follow signs from the universe, but I just am not sure about this one. But I can't back out now. That would be rude, and I am not rude. I am a nice person, and I usually give everyone a chance. I am sure he is a nice person, her brother Ben. I just don't want to go. Usually I go with the flow, but not this time. Ugh, I need to change my attitude. I don't want to be cold and closed. That's not fair to him."

Approaching noon, I start to get nervous as Hope's still talking out loud to herself in front of the mirror. I see her, and she definitely needs to take a shower and clean up her act. Yesterday, she lay low, as she does most weekends these days. Her healthy side keeps saying out loud, "Hope, this is good. It will get you out of the apartment and give you a chance to breathe in some fresh air."

She knows the importance of connecting with nature, especially because she lives in this concrete jungle. Her weekend routine usually starts with grabbing a Grande Passion Tazo tea and heading to Central Park. That is her favorite spot in Manhattan. She jumps on the MTA subway, rides to Seventy-Second Street, and then walks to Strawberry Fields, which is a two-and-a-half-acre landscaped section in Central Park. That area is dedicated to the memory of former Beatles member John Lennon. We met at that spot for walks on the weekends so that we could recap our wins and losses of the week. One of our favorite songs in high school was "Imagine" by John Lennon. Even at an early age, we were moved by that song, which wasn't a predictable favorite for a high school student in our time. Although, our friendship was never typical. Usually, friends come and go, or the relationship ebbs and flows. But not us, we stuck close.

At one point, Hope had an opportunity to move to Santa Cruz, but she decided not to take it. One of the reasons was that she would miss being around me. Sounds foolish, and she knew that I would have supported her leaving, but there are some people in your life that you want close by. I was one of those people for her.

But now, *I* left *her*. And I was nowhere in sight…until now.

But how do I let her know I am right here next to her?

When Ben texted Hope about a mutually convenient meeting, Central Park was the first thing that came to her mind. After Hope sent the recommendation for the meeting spot, she later regretted it. She said out loud, "Why did I do that?" Her mind went off on a tangent, and she started thinking about all the emotions that may arise just by being back at her favorite place where she'd shared so many memories with her best friend. It was too late to change the meeting place; the date was in about ninety minutes.

Hope jumped in the shower and continued to contemplate what to wear for her Central Park date. While the conditioner was in her hair, she decided on a casual look. Since it was a sunny spring day, the final decision was a nice pair of jeans—not the ones with the hole in the knee—a flowery top with bright colors, and comfy sandals. She kept it simple because that was all that she could handle for the day. The date itself was already a stretch.

As she left the apartment, Hope said, "Grace, I had to pick out my outfit alone. I hope I made you proud." With her voice cracking, she continued, "It would be great if you could just be here with me. God knows, I could use your support." This was the first time Hope had spoken to her departed bestie out loud; she couldn't find the courage to admit that I was really gone and not coming back any time soon, if ever.

Ben is waiting in front of a park bench; he's wearing a tan wind-breaker and jeans. People are laughing, and kids are running around the park. The vibe is full of joy and play. It is a perfect sunny day, not a cloud in the sky. You can smell the crispness in the air; fall is now officially here. The trees are changing by the day. Bright yellows, reds, and oranges surround him. Football season is in full effect.

Hope arrives five minutes late, which is typical. She was never great with time. When she first lays eyes on Ben, my bestie is pleas-antly surprised. He has kind eyes, soft and bright.

Ben recognizes Hope as she approaches and greets her with a smile. He holds out his hand and says, "Nice to meet you, Hope. Glad we could meet today. What a beautiful day!"

Hope looks a little thrown off by the handshake because she is more of a hugger, but she goes with it and offers her hand.

I know what she is thinking. That's how close we were. And she, deep down, knows that it's her stuff she's projecting when things come up lately, and she knows it's not fair to dump her baggage on a stranger. She's in her forties, so let's just say she's not a quick study, and she's had plenty of opportunities to learn during all her dating adventures, which were with men all across the board—older, younger, white collar, blue collar, different races, and different religions. For her, it was more about the energy of the connection.

Maybe Ben is a little different from her usual type. He seems plain, vanilla. All Hope knows is that he comes from an upper-middle-class family from a suburb of Long Island, New York; he's employed and lives in the Upper West Side. She is glad that his sister didn't share many details; she wants to make her own assessment.

Hope shakes Ben's hand and with a shy smile says, "Ben, nice to meet you as well."

As they started walking, Ben starts the conversation, "So my sister says that you have lived in the city for a while. Do you come to this part of the park often?"

Hope takes a deep breath and answers. "Yes, this is one of my favorite places to go in the city."

Is she thinking about all the times she and I came here? I am glad she didn't elaborate. I'm emotional right now, and as sensitive as Hope is, she might fall into tears. Not good on a first date.

Finally, after a few minutes of silence that felt like an eternity, Hope asked, "How about you? You like living in the city?"

Ben looked relieved, like he was thinking, *Finally a question from her!* "I've lived in the Upper West Side for most of the time, except for when I first moved to Manhattan. Five of my college friends, including me, squeezed into a two-bedroom where the landlord put up a couple of partitions, so we each could have our own space. We stayed there for two years; in many ways, I loved those times. But now, the thought of sharing a place with four other guys, at this time in my life, would not work for me. I am happy to have more space, so I have been living in the same one-bedroom apartment for five years; it's about 850 square feet. The time has gone fast. It still feels like home."

Hope lit up a bit, identifying with what Ben was saying. "I understand. I have been in my studio for close to ten years. People tell me all the time to move and upgrade. Like you, I feel that it is my home. I love my neighbors; they are my extended family."

Ben suddenly got distracted and pointed to the side of the path, where flowers were in bloom and three butterflies were hovering.

Hope got choked up and couldn't disguise her feelings.

Ben looked at her with concern. "Hope, are you okay?"

Hope fessed up about what was going on with her emotionally. "Brittany might have mentioned that my best friend died six months ago. We used to watch the butterflies in the park and were fascinated by how beautiful they were. We would talk about how they originated from a cocoon and then transformed into exquisite creatures who could fly. You mentioning that made me think of her. I am still incredibly sad; she was my best friend since the eighth grade. It has been a big adjustment, moving forward without her."

Ben felt bad, and it was written all over his face.

Hope said, "Look, you didn't know. Actually, no one else knows about that. I'm sorry; maybe it was a mistake to come. I am a bit of a mess these days. But I didn't want to be rude and cancel. I know your sister mentioned this a while back."

Ben, with kind eyes, said, "I am so sorry. She told me a little bit about it, but didn't really know the extent of your loss. I didn't realize that you were friends back in junior high school. Was she like a sister to you?"

The tears ran down Hope's face. "Yes, she was. I grew up with two brothers, and she was the closest female figure to me, besides my mom and grandmother."

I was watching and felt the pain coming from my best friend. I felt such emptiness. I was so busy figuring out my journey that I didn't realize how hard this would be for Hope. What could I do to alleviate some of the pain? What could I do to bring some peace to my dear friend? And then I had it, an idea. Finding solutions was always my thing.

I closed my eyes and thought of Enzo. And in an instant, he was there, with me in Central Park. I was getting good at asking for help and relying on him to be there. I never before trusted men to be there. When I needed them desperately, I would demand from them. With that energy, they never would come; it was almost as though they ignored my panicking plea.

With a big smile, Enzo said, "Hello, Grace, can I help?"

Excited about the idea, I spoke with enthusiasm, "Actually, you can. I am getting better at asking for what I need. Finally getting the hang of it."

He chuckled and made light of things, especially about earthly issues. This was a serious matter for me, a huge transformational shift. Being open to allowing others to help me was a huge step for me. It was part of my soul's lesson and would help me move forward.

I continued, "Enzo, could we round up some butterflies and have them fly around Hope now? This may let her know that I am here supporting and loving her."

"You got it, Grace."

He had the three butterflies fly around Ben and Hope. He even had one land on Hope's hand. Next, he raised his hands, with palms out, and I sensed a sudden wave of calming, peaceful energy that I'm sure ran through both Ben and Hope too.

Hope looked down at her hand and asked Ben, "Did you feel that?"

He paused before answering, "Yes, I did. I've never felt anything like that. Have you?"

Hope, still feeling a sense of tranquility, replied, "No, I guess there is a first time for everything. I can't believe that three butterflies were flying around us. One even landed on my hand. It's weird because Grace and I would come to the park and be on the lookout for butter-flies. We always saw more of them when we were going through a significant change—say, starting a new job, leaving an apartment, or even being in a new intimate relationship."

Ben asked, "Would you like to grab a tea or green drink?"

Hope asked, "No coffee?"

Ben quickly responded, "Oh sure, if you like. I took you more for a tea or green-drink person."

Hope smiled. "You're right. Let's go get me a green tea, decaf if possible."

As they headed out of the park, Hope looked at the sky and said softly, "Hi, Gracey, thanks for being with me on this first date."

I responded, "You are most welcome, bestie. And you did good with the outfit." My hope was that she heard me.

♡

Exploration Questions
Chapter 9

Hope

1. Who was your best friend growing up and/or in high school? Are you still in touch?

2. Who is your closest friend today? Or do you have a couple? A tribe?

3. How has your best friend supported you through various relationships?

4. What have you told your best friend that you have not told anyone else?

5. Grace and Hope are very different and remained extremely close. In what ways are you and your closest friend alike and different?

Chapter 9 Activity

Bond with Your Bestie: Share this book with your best friend (if you haven't already), and get their feedback to the questions at the end of each chapter.

Chapter 10

Little Enzo

I'm back with Enzo, and I have tons of questions for him. It's important I get information here. I need to make sure that Hope will be okay. I'm concerned for her and want to make sure that her future is bright. I've been so consumed with my journey; it didn't dawn on me how much my passing would impact her. Witnessing Hope's mourning further solidified that I've mattered; in life, I did not always feel that I really was valued. From time to time, people would tell me that I was, but I did not always believe it.

What I am discovering is my true worth and sense of self. It is not about relying on others to give me validation. I always felt like the more I needed, the less other people gave. I am uncovering that I have much more love and strength within than I thought. When I was on Earth it was always about going outside myself to feel acknowledged, especially when it came to men.

"So is Hope going to find love? I totally left her, and now I am worried. Will she get married and have kids? She is not one for a conventional life, but maybe some stability would be helpful?"

Enzo smiled and touched my shoulder. "She will be simply fine. Grace, you don't need to protect her; she has everything she needs for her journey. Let me show you something." Enzo put his hand on my back and said, "Close your eyes, and look within. See Hope; look into the future."

I closed my eyes and could see Hope on a cliff overlooking a beautiful sea, the sun shining bright. There she is, in a Bohemian white dress holding a bouquet of white roses with a lilac bow. She is glowing and looks stunning. Her dress is so simple and yet elegant. Just the kind of thing I would have helped her choose.

Was she thinking of me when she picked it out?

Hope looks joyfully at her soon-to-be husband. It's Ben, that guy from the park. When I first saw him, I knew he was a good one. I could see it in his eyes.

A few close family and friends are seated in white chairs facing the couple. There's Hope's neighbor Anna right in the front. Hope loves her as if she were her own grandmother. I feel peaceful watching this scene unfold, knowing that Hope will find happiness and is surrounded by people who care for her, maybe as much as I did. I still do and always will.

Enzo prompts, "That's not all. Keep your eyes closed and see."

There is a little girl, three years old with pigtails and in overalls. She is running towards Hope. Hope has her arms wide open, and the little girl jumps into them and laughs. With her big brown eyes, she looks at her mother, smiles, and says, "Hi, Mommy!"

"Hi, Gracey!"

Hope's destiny was to be a mom, and my friend has honored my soul by naming her little one after me. I know in my heart that I will always be remembered by my bestie and soul sister, Hope. I am speechless, which is a quite rarity, because I always had unanswered questions, a by-product of my curious mind.

"Thank you, Enzo, for showing me this. I feel complete, and Hope is more than okay. I guess the assignment was to be there on her first date. I am getting that somehow my presence made her feel my support, even though she could not see me in the flesh."

"You are catching on quicker and quicker as each task is completed. Hope almost didn't go on that date, and once she got there, she almost walked away. She saw Ben, and Hope thought about what you would say to her if you knew that she was going to bail. 'Hope, give the guy a shot. He was on time, he's at your favorite park, and you did shower for the event.' Even though she couldn't see you, she was channeling your spirit. She realized it first unconsciously, and then when she saw the butterflies, she consciously knew you were there. That was when Hope intuitively decided to stay, be present, and more open. She wanted to make you proud that she was being more vulnerable."

I grinned. "Vulnerability was never our strong suit. We prided ourselves in being strong, independent women. Being vulnerable was never easy; we could do it with each other and be open and real. We always made fun of ourselves about how much we sucked at it when it came to dating. We would joke that was why we were soul sistahs."

Enzo continued, "Because you are changing, you are shifting your energy. It is stronger now; it gave Hope the strength to put herself out there more. And look, she ended up marrying a wonderful guy and having a child too. That would not have been possible if you weren't present at her most vulnerable moment. You know she had little to no desire to go on that first date. Even when she showed up, she was ready to leave the second she got to the park. It was not about Ben; it was about her. Her ability to receive and stay. That defining moment changed her path, and she started to open up, even if it was just a small crack at first. That opening was all that she needed to proceed and go on the next date and the next. Each date built the intimacy that was necessary to eventually lead to marriage."

I listened quietly. Every word out of his mouth really resonated with me. "How did you get so good at this, or even land this job?"

He replied after a big, gruff laugh, "I have failed many times, but each time I dusted myself off and tried again to get where I am now."

Enzo continued, "I was a neglected kid that lived in the inner city. My family was poor, and my father struggled to keep a job. My mom did the best she could, making the food stretch for five kids, but there were nights I went to bed hungry. I was the third child, so I got lost in the pack. I wandered the streets all the time and skipped school. I felt that there was no reason to go; it was a big waste of time. I was kind of an asshole with a chip on my shoulder most days.

"Except when it came to my little brother. I was always good to him. Every ounce of my kindness went into that kid. I loved my little brother, Michael. We called him Mikey. He was the youngest and always looked up to me. He had such beautiful, big blue eyes that looked at the world with such innocence and wonder. This was surprising because he was born in that crummy neighborhood where we lived and into a messed-up family. As he got older, he never left my side, except when I made him go to school. He had to go. I wanted better for him. He was smart; he picked up reading, writing, and math with no problem.

"We didn't have much of a father, and when Pop *was* around, he went straight to the bottle. We had a life my father wanted to forget every day, and my mom always made excuses for him. So I was the father figure for Mikey, and I took pride in that. He would jump off the couch with excitement to go to the store with me. His eyes showed such joy every time I'd give him an extra piece of candy. I made some money on the side, running errands to help make ends meet, and I always made sure I put aside some for Mikey's candy fund.

"I was an angry kid; I couldn't shake how much of a raw deal we kids got in this world. My rage never went away. If anything, it expanded as I got older, taking up more space. I got caught up with a mob leader who was collecting protection money from local businesses, selling drugs, and making those who got in his way 'disappear.' I was delivering messages and packages all over the city for him. I never knew what I was movin' in those envelopes. But deep down, I knew it was no good and not making the neighborhood a safer, better place. The boss appreciated my work ethic and got a kick out of my smart-aleck attitude. I knew better than to use it on him, though. I did have *some* common sense; I wasn't *that* stupid. I was quick and knew the neighborhood like the back of my hand. I knew to not ask questions, to just do what was asked of me. No commentary, no pushback, just make the drop-off, and get out of there.

"From time to time, Mikey would come with me on deliveries. I liked having the kid around. At first, the boss was not on board with Mikey hanging around while I was making my rounds. He wanted nothin' or no one getting in the way of his business on the streets. One day, when he was in a good mood, he had a change in attitude; he took a liking to Mikey, recognized his sweetness and innocence. I should have realized he saw that as an opportunity to manipulate and exploit. It was an opportunity to groom someone else to help him build his empire. He only saw Mikey as another pawn on his chessboard, someone to do the dirty work. The boss was very cunning and manipulative, and he preyed on the weak.

"Mikey just wanted to be part of the pack, play with the big boys, be one of us. That kid always looked up to me. I was the only person in his life that really had his back. Absent father, broken mother, our brothers and sisters were barely getting by themselves and had no time for him. I was his person, and he was mine. The kid made me feel like I was actually worth something in this world. I never thought much of myself and knew I made trouble for people. I hated the disgust I felt every time my Pop walked in the door drunk, and part of me was disgusted with myself. I could see parts of Pop in me when I looked in the mirror. We shared that same anger and rage. When Mikey looked at me, I saw the love he had for me. He didn't look at me with disgust or disappointment. I was never gonna take that for granted. I would have done anything for my little brother—even die for him.

"One day when I was makin' rounds, I left Mikey with the boss. I only had a couple stops, so it was an easy day. The boss said he would watch him while I finished my route. I was skeptical and said, 'You sure?'

"The boss said, 'Yeah, I got this; I'll watch him.' Hearing that, Mikey's eyes filled with excitement because he knew that staying with the boss was a big deal. He wanted people to see him as someone who could hang, even at the ripe age of eleven years old. He wanted to be part of the crowd, part of the happenings. I always worried about him because he had such an innocence about him. He was so naïve.

"I hadn't been innocent since I was eight. The first time I saw my father come home drunk and knock my mom around, my sense of security vanished. That's when I really lost respect for my pop. And I no longer felt safe in my own home. This happened a couple of times a week, especially on late nights when he was at the bar with his buddies. I protected Mikey as best I could from seeing that stuff. The nights I knew my pop would be coming home from the pub, I'd make sure to get us outa the house.

"We would head to the park, or a friend's house when we could, and Mikey would fall asleep on my lap. When I thought it was safe to go back to the house, I would carry him home and put him to bed. By then, Pop would be passed out drunk, and Mom would be asleep. I did everything to protect that innocence; it is what made him a kid, made him special.

"When I walked out the door that day, I looked at Mikey and the boss, and knew deep down leaving him there was a bad idea. I told myself, *It's just for a little while. I'll be right back. What could go wrong? And it makes Mikey feel like one of the guys.* But I didn't listen to my gut. I may not have been the brightest guy in the room, but I had good instincts. I just thought, *Let me do these three last deliveries, and I'll be done for the day.* I would buy Mikey a cone from the ice-cream truck and enjoy the rest of the hot summer evening. His favorite flavor was chocolate with chocolate sprinkles on top. By the end, half the ice cream would be all over his shirt because he couldn't lick it faster than it melted. That always cracked me up.

"While I was out, the boss decided to send Mikey out on an errand. Mikey was thrilled. He jumped at the chance. 'Sure I can do it. I promise I won't let you down.' If I had known that any of that would happen, I would not have let him out of my sight. I should have known better. All the money from the deliveries meant nothing. Being Mikey's brother was the only thing in my life that really mattered.

"Mikey was supposed to go pick up an envelope at an abandoned apartment building just a block away. He was so excited that he actually skipped the whole way over. When he got there, he was met by a young dude, skinny, not much older than me at the time. This guy was known for being a bully, a brute. He had a mean streak and a rep for giving people a hard time, an asshole. But he never messed with me. The guy knew I could destroy him if he provoked me even a little bit. Everybody knew about my rage.

"I never knew what really went down. On my way back to the warehouse, I turned the corner in front of the apartment, and there was Mikey. His spiritless body, laying in the gutter, covered in blood. There was a little girl there, too, crouched down in the street, holding his hand. He was faceup, with his eyes closed.

"I ran over to see if he was still breathing. 'Please God!' I begged. 'Let me see his chest move.' I pulled him into my lap one last time, hot tears streaming down my face. 'What happened?' I screamed at the little girl.

"'I dunno. I just saw him on my way home from the store.'

"I could tell he was hurt, so I ran back in the store and asked Mr. Girardi to call the ambulance. But I didn't want to leave Mikey alone 'til they got there. I went back outside.

"The little girl was still there, and she said, 'So I've just been talking to him. It'll be all right, Mister. Hear the sirens? The ambulance is already on the way. It'll be all right.'

"This tiny little girl, no older than Mikey, was being the strong one. She didn't even flinch as I cried and screamed my prayers to God. I never talked to God, but this was a time I did. And there was my rage, in full form. I hadn't kept my promise to protect Mikey. This was my fault for bringing him into my dirty world. All I ever wanted to do was protect his innocence, but all I did was destroy it. Destroy him.

"I couldn't get my breath. I was gasping for air and struggling to get the words out of my mouth. 'Help us! Help us!' I feared I was too late as I cradled his motionless body. I looked up at the sky and prayed. I prayed with every ounce of my being. 'God, I'll do anything to save his life, anything! This is *my* fault. How can I fix this? Take me, God! Take me instead!'

"When I looked into the little girl's eyes, she had the same innocence as Mikey. She was a sweet little angel and was there for my Mikey."

Enzo paused, but figured that Grace was still processing all of this, so he decided to continue. "Suddenly, a bright golden light came over us, the most beautiful light I had ever seen before. I looked at the little girl, an angel in a flowered cotton dress, the hem stained with Mikey's blood, her eyes as innocent as Mikey's. And I heard a deep voice say, 'Loving Enzo, I will grant your prayer. You may exchange your life for his. Your spirit journey now has been changed forever. This will be your last life on Earth. You will join my team in the heavens and will guide others.'

"The little girl just looked at Mikey, like she hadn't heard the voice at all. The color was coming back to his face. I could see him take a breath, and his eyes fluttered. Weakly, he stammered, 'Where am I?'

"I started to cry tears of joy. It was a miracle. Like, a right-outa-the-Bible miracle. And in that moment, I knew that Mikey would be okay.

"The little girl looked up at me, excited, 'Told ya! I knew he would be...'

"*But why is she looking at me like that?* I wondered. *Why is she afraid now? Everything's okay now, right?* And then I felt it, not even for a second. Just a hot, hot feeling in my chest. I thought my heart might be exploding with relief and joy, but no...

"I felt like I needed to protect the little girl too. The skinny dude had come back, to finish the job, finish me. What a bastard, or I guess I should say troubled soul."

"Wow, Enzo, I feel like I know this story. As you were telling it, it's like I was right there, like I had seen this in a movie before or something. It was so real and so familiar. Weird."

"Well, that's because you were there, Grace. You were that little girl…just in another life."

"Ah! This is when we knew each other. I get it!"

Enzo replied, "Yes, it was your soul. Obviously, it was not you as Grace, but as another person. Again, this was years ago. Our souls are reborn many times. It is part of our journey and transformation. We decide what body and lifetime we want to experience. We choose based on what lessons we need to learn that will help us reach a higher level of consciousness. We travel in soul clusters, with others who help us grow and transform.

"You helped Mikey, which means you helped me. I was nowhere to be found when Mikey got shot. And you were there; he did not have to suffer alone. Your presence supported him and me. And now I am helping you. Make sense?"

"You know, it actually does."

"I know that God sent you to be there and get Mikey help. I'm now on a journey of service. It was a life for a life. You were with me when I got shot. And when you were hit by a car, I was there to greet you. I wanted you to feel the peace I did.

"As a spirit, I was still able to watch Mikey grow up. I saw him walk across the stage when he graduated high school. I came back when my father took his last breath, despite all the anger and resentment I always had for him. I might have saved Mikey's life, but he saved my soul. I've helped souls and continue to experience myself in a way that I never thought was possible. I am a good soul who makes a difference. If I could be saved and changed, then anyone can be. It was the grace of God that healed my soul, and now I provide the space for others to heal and transform."

I am moved when I hear Enzo's story. I understand why he feels familiar. I had met him before, although I had no memory of it. I wonder if helping other souls transform impacts Enzo's soul as well. I'm beginning to understand why God has linked him to me. What is it about my soul that needs his presence, though? Instead of overanalyzing it, as I normally would, I ask him directly and get straight to the point. "Enzo, why did you pick me? Why did you want to be my guide? Is this what brought us together?"

"You and me, we have a lot of similarities. We have an edge, we are straightforward, and we don't trust much. I am helping you to do that. Trust yourself. And I feel indebted to you. You were there for my Mikey and me, and I will always be grateful. I got your back now. Let's move on. Now it's time for your next adventure."

I had no idea what would be next, because I had a long list of boyfriends Enzo could want me to either visit or work through issues with.

"Grace, remember this is about you, not them. You have all the answers. It is within you."

Truthfully, I'm finally getting it and learning to embrace me. It is about my being more reflective and discovering my own answers without picking up a book or asking someone else. Now I know it's time to continue my quest, my journey. I'm getting closer to my goal and learning my lessons, which makes me proud.

"What's next, Enzo? Or is the more accurate question, who is next?"

♡

Exploration Questions
Chapter 10
Little Enzo

1. Enzo is quite the character. Have you known anyone like him—gruff on the outside, but a real marshmallow underneath? Do you think Enzo's childhood tragedy makes him a good guide in the afterlife?

2. How has your family impacted the way you love yourself and others?

3. What did you learn about love as a child?

4. How has your upbringing shaped who you are?

5. What relatives who are no longer living would you like to see again and why?

Chapter 10 Activity

Design a Family Tree: Gather pictures, and use either poster board or an online app to create a "tree" with everyone's photos. This is a fun project to share with other family members. Reach out to one family member to whom you haven't spoken in a while.

Chapter 11

Liam

*H*ere *we go again!* It happens in a flash. You'd think by now I'd be used to being transported from one place to another. There hasn't been any rhyme or reason, except each relationship was a significant one in which I learned about an aspect of myself. Usually, I can figure it out fairly quickly. This time, it took a bit longer.

This assignment is unlike the others; there's no familiarity. I usually pick up on surroundings or the person. Nope, not this time. I have no clue, although I am learning to go more with the flow. Normally, I would put the pressure on and be upset if I did not have a problem solved in the first few minutes. I have to say, this process has taught me a few extraordinary qualities, especially patience. Funny that I had to die to learn that one. *At least I still have my sense of humor.*

I find myself in an old living room, or maybe a study, with a wall of built-in bookshelves and a fire burning brightly. There's a white-haired gentleman talking to, it seems, his grandsons. Perhaps in his late seventies, he's wearing an old Bruins sweatshirt stretched over a little bit of a gut. His grandsons look like either high school seniors or maybe college freshmen, and they are seated in two wingback chairs facing him.

"Sean and Patrick, as you both go on to college, note there will be lots of women and plenty of alcohol. Enjoy yourselves. I did. Let me tell you a story about me. It was a moment in time when I was about your age. Will you promise not to share this story with your mom? I never go into the details of other women around her. Well, it would be quite awkward because your nana is your mom's mom. You know women; they stick together. So there is no need to ruffle any feathers or piss anyone off, especially since your nana is not around anymore and was a wonderful wife, mother, and nana to all of you. Although, prior to meeting your nana, there was a special lady in my life. One that I've always remembered; our connection has stayed with me throughout my life."

One of the grandsons asked, "If she was so special, why didn't you marry her?"

"Well, that's a good question, but sometimes it just isn't in the cards. Plus, there are times you blow it big-time and kill the opportunity. She was mine for a summer, but in the end, we went our separate ways. I knew it was completely over when I met your nana. At the time, it was clear I was meant to be with your nana, and then we had your uncles, and of course your mom.

"I did keep in touch with this lady from time to time, but more through social media because she had her life, and I had mine. She went to college in a different state. I mean, it was in New England, so looking back, not far. At the time, it seemed miles away.

"She was my first real love, and I believe I was hers as well. I was irresistible. Back in the day, I had a great full head of hair. She captivated me from the beginning. I knew I wanted to be around her the minute I laid eyes on her. I enjoyed her sarcastic way; this girl was witty, smart. She had a smile that charmed me, and I appreciated that she never took my shit. You know how I am. I'm a piece of work."

His grandsons acknowledge that by nodding. They knew their grandfather was a handful. He was usually getting into some trouble, although it was usually harmless.

"My parents felt that your nana had the patience of a saint. I married her for it. I think that was the only decision my parents, your great-grandparents, approved of in my life. I don't think that they thought a good woman would put up with me. Which bothered me a bit, but whatever; that's in the past."

He continued, "My parents insisted that I have a job for the summer. Truth was, my work ethic sucked. I was more about playing hockey than about making a nominal amount of money from a part-time gig. I did McDonald's one year, retail the next, and the best one was being a waiter at a catering hall. I spent a lot of time eating the leftovers from weddings, sweet-sixteen parties, and bar mitzvahs. Being on my feet and having to work really hard was not in my DNA. My parents were threatening me at the time; if I could not hold a job for the summer, they wouldn't let me go to the University of New Hampshire. All I wanted to do is be out on my own, no curfew, party, and play club hockey. The only way they would allow me to go to UNH was for me to hold a part-time job for the entire summer. You think, 'How could you fuck that up,' but as a kid, I had a way of turning a good thing into a disaster."

As this man is telling the story, I am lurking in the background. It is kind of creepy that I can see them, but they can't see me. This time, no one notices me, unlike other times, with Grayson and his daughter, or even Matty. I am still perplexed and racking my brain, trying to figure out who these people are and why I am here. And that's when I hear my name.

"My first love was Grace. Her full name was Grace Isabella Anderson. And boy, she was a beauty."

Now I am slowly recognizing the voice; it's familiar, but I can't put my finger on it quite yet. I continue to focus and anxiously wait to see how the story unfolds. It seems to be about me, so eventually my questions will be answered, and it will register. For now, my curiosity is piqued as I stand in the corner, surrounded by shelves of hardcover books and family photos.

"…Watermill Terrace…"

What did he just say? Now I get it. *Liam, it is you. My Liam. How you have changed physically, yet your energy feels the same.*

I feel myself tearing up at being here with such a special person in my life. I'm taken back to a time in my life when I learned so much about myself. I always had a soft spot when I heard from him, although it was not often. I knew he met someone right after we went our separate ways and was married while still in his twenties.

I appreciated how I could be myself with Liam, and that was a rarity with other men after him. I never understood why it was different with Liam. I chalked it up to his just giving me the space to do me. Nothing more, nothing less. Looking back, it was a gift for me that lasted my entire life…and even into the afterlife, it seems. Although I am indeed perplexed as to why on Earth—no pun intended—I'm here in his study. I imagine Liam calls it his man cave. I left no loose ends and never looked back after we went our separate ways.

So many of the other encounters have been about learning about myself. But I'm unclear why I've been sent to Liam. Enzo always has a reason for my time travels and choosing whom I meet along the way. The good news is that I'm more patient now with this process, more trusting of the journey.

But Liam looks so old and not well physically. He seems tired, and his coloring is sallow. Perhaps, he is sick. There's a huge flannel quilt covering his legs, even though I can see red sweatpants, thick socks, and slippers sticking out the bottom. He was never a fashionista. He always needed a bit of help with his clothing. Even when he tried one time to dress up for our official date, his pants were wrinkled, his shoes a bit worn, and his shirt did not exactly match the overall look. I silently appreciated the gesture of his version of dressing up. For Liam, not to wear jeans or shorts was a big deal. It was his version of stepping up and showing he was into it. He was not a showman, not into any sort of flash, but if he made an effort to dress up for a girl, that was a big deal. This was a guy who did not even put on a button-down for the prom; he was never into tradition or making a fuss over life's milestones.

That is why I loved him. Liam was unconventional; his way of seeing the world was unique and on his own terms. I admired him for that; he did not care what people thought of him. People, especially his mom and dad, saw Liam as defiant, but I saw him from another angle. I admired his gumption.

Liam continued sharing how we met during the summer we were eighteen years old. The grandsons are clearly interested in his story. Perhaps they know that the end is in sight and want to spend some extra time with their favorite grandpa. I am assuming he's their favorite. I could see Liam giving them many firsts. Sitting in box seats at a Bruins game, sneaking them a sip of beer—he probably let them drink the entire bottle—when they were underage, and letting them drive around the parking lot when they barely could see over the steering wheel. He always pushed the envelope and somehow got away with it. I am sure that they loved him for that. I know most children don't experience their grandfathers in this way, but both Liam and I experienced a special bond with our grandfathers. I bet, secretly, Liam was happy when they were both born boys. If they were girls, what would he say or do with them? For him, it probably was much easier to relate to boys.

Liam continues, "Well, let me tell you about Grace, Gracey. She did not always like it when I called her that. It fired her up." Liam chuckled as he remembered. "She always said that I would call her that when I wanted to get a rise out of her and test her patience." He laughs again. "She may have been right about that. She made straight As, always had her nose in a book, and at times challenged the status quo. Secretly, that is the side that I liked about her. It was not easy for her to do; whereas, for me, it was second nature. I thrived on causing upheaval; it was my drug of choice. Okay, *one* of my addictions."

Liam smiled again as he continued sharing his memory. "I met her on that summer job that my parents made me get, the one I had to keep in order to prove that I was capable of responsibility. I had to pass their 'responsibility test'; otherwise, instead of going to the UNH, I was commuting to community college in a hand-me-down Honda Accord that your Uncle Finn drove his freshman year. That could not happen to this kid. This guy? No way, no how!"

Sean interrupted and asked, "So how long did it take for you to lose the job?"

In reply, Liam just smiled.

I could see that his grandsons knew him well, especially that Sean. He was the most like Liam in looks and personality. I observed that Patrick was a bit quieter.

"Deep down, I knew that I wasn't really adept at the time. My parents were right in a lot of ways, although I would never admit it, especially as an eighteen-year-old. However, somehow, I was able to squeak through and hold the job for the summer. Your great-grandpa got me the job at this catering hall called Watermill Terrace. Through work, he knew a guy who knew a guy that owned this catering business and needed help for the summer. Weddings and family functions were big during the summer months, and this was one of the hottest places to go on Long Island.

"Let me tell you, it was hard work. You were on your feet from 4:00 p.m. until midnight or 1:00 a.m. There was cocktail hour, then first course; after that was main course, and the grand finale was the Venetian hour. It is a delicious and filling Italian wedding tradition. That was when the catering staff wheels out a plethora of desserts for the guests to choose from. It is held towards the end of a wedding. A large buffet of pastries, cakes, fruits, ice cream and sorbet flavors, liqueurs, and coffee are served along with the wedding cake.

"There was always so much excess that all the workers indulged as we were cleaning up for the night. That is when I was introduced to my favorite dessert, tiramisu, and cannoli is a close second. I always had the taste of an Italian.

"I started at the end of June, the weekend after my senior year of high school. I rolled in a bit disheveled because I went out the night before with a few buddies to celebrate the end of world as we knew it. We were all excited about what the world had in store for us. Three out of my five close buddies were going away to school in the fall, so that summer was our last hurrah together.

"I knew I needed to get my act together since I did not want to lose my job on the first day. That would be an all-time low for even me at the time. I was already annoyed because, prior to my arriving at the catering hall, I had to buy a certain kind of white shirt, black dress pants, and a black bow tie, which was completely ridiculous-looking. But that was the uniform we were required to wear. I was never a shirt-and-tie kind of person, let alone one to wear a tuxedo-looking outfit. Again, I could suck it up because the goal was to get by so I could go to UNH. I had to keep my eye on the prize!

"On my first day, as I tucked in my shirt and stumbled through the door, I saw a group of people, say anywhere from seventeen to twenty-five years old, that were dressed like me, waiting to hear what our assignments would be for the night. I looked around and thought, *Maybe this won't be so bad; at least these people are my age. I can hang with them after work, grab a beer or something.*

"And then I saw her, she caught my eye right away. Grace walked in, her brown hair, half up, a bit wavy; she was wearing what looked like a maid's dress. Black and white, a bit below the knees. Suddenly, I did not feel so bad about my outfit. The women had to be in uniforms as well; they had it way worse than the guy's.

"So instead of going up to her and introducing myself, I did what?"

Sean said, "You, of course, avoided her."

Liam said, "Yes, that's right. I did exactly that. She even came over and smiled at me. Instead of having some balls and saying hi, I acted like I did not see her come by. I acted distracted. Yeah, I know—rookie move."

As he was talking about it, I see both Sean and Patrick roll their eyes and shake their heads.

"Then the person in charge, who was a real ass, started giving us a speech about how this club was the most prestigious in Long Island and that it was all about the customer experience…blah, blah, blah. And then he assigned us all our jobs for the night, and that was the last I saw of Grace that evening. The job was quite hard. I was constantly being directed to do this and that for the event. I was so exhausted by midnight that I went straight home, no hanging out with coworkers. And, believe it or not, I did not even desire a beer. Although I was happy to be only a twenty-minute drive from home.

"During the next couple of weeks, I was helping out with all sorts of events. Setting up the room, waiting tables, and running errands to make sure the event went off without a hitch. The good news is that I got tips.

"Some old, drunk men would be bored and start talking to me about sports. When I mentioned that I wanted to play hockey at UNH, they perked up. They were die-hard Islander fans. Poor fellows, that team was strong for only two years, better for them to root for the Rangers, but people have their own cross to bear. I was always a Bruins fan. I felt I was born with the New England gene. I liked most New England teams, which was uncommon living in Long Island. People looked at me with disdain when I mentioned anything about the Red Sox. In Long Island, they were all about their Mets. Why they didn't transfer their love of the game and become Yankee fans…I'll never understand the thought process there. I guess they were gluttons for punishment. Okay, I digress. Let's get back to Grace.

"Come mid-July, Grace and I were finally working the same event. It was a 300-person wedding, a huge event, all hands on deck. Most of the employees were there, and we were lectured to be on our best behavior, especially since the press was covering the event. The wedding was for the daughter of a highly influential CEO in Long Island. They handed out our assignments; Grace and I were covering the same areas. I was pretty excited about it, but did my best to act cool and show I did not care a bit. You know you can't let a lady know. My face was stoic and void of feeling, although inside I was stoked!"

With a confused look Patrick said, "Stoked?"

Liam responded, "Excited."

Patrick nodded.

Liam continued the story, "I remember that hall; it had not just one, but four huge chandeliers that spread throughout the four sections of the room. The room tastefully whispered opulence, especially when the sunlight beamed throughout it. How that light brought joy to every event that happened in that space. It overlooked a man-made lake with a fountain, and how it sparkled at the start of a special evening. It was a magical, romantic room, and I don't even like the glitz and glamour. No need to go into more detail.

"Anyway, our manager calls names out for the first assignment, which is the cocktail-food station. He proceeds to announce the first name, which is mine, next is Jennifer, and the one after was Grace, beautiful Gracey. Serving crab cakes, shrimp cocktail, and mini beef Wellingtons was really when we met for the first time. I finally got some balls and greeted her right away with a hi and a slight smile."

As he is telling the story, I am enthralled. It was so interesting to hear his perspective. It was so different than I remembered it. Liam always held a soft spot in my heart; he was my first in so many ways. I was eighteen when I met him. He was the first person with whom I could really be myself. He was simple and had an edge. I knew he adored me from the start. His energy made me feel very comfortable; he was home to me. He was drawn to beer, sports, and, well, girls too. I was more of an intellect; Bookworm was one of his favorite nick-names with which he fondly teased me since he always saw me with a book in my bag or in my hand. I knew that is what Liam liked about me; I was so different than him.

He told me the last time he really read a book from cover to cover was late in his junior year of high school, and really the reason he read it from cover to cover was because Michelle, who sat in front of him, was raving about it with a fellow classmate. He had a crush on her, and he knew he would have to have something to talk about to get her attention. So he read it, but the flirtation only lasted a few weeks. I knew Liam was simple, but not dumb. He could bring on the charm when he wanted to.

When it came to sex with Liam, he actually was my first. At the time, I was a bit nervous about the entire experience. The questions flooding my mind were *will it hurt? will I like it?* and *will he enjoy himself?* My excitement turned to anxiety. But when we came to that moment, I felt safe with Liam, and I was grateful that he was my first. That intimacy was precious, and I never forgot it. Although the relationship didn't last, luckily, I had no regrets.

I am interested in hearing how he tells the story of us, because our ending was a bit abrupt and had one or two loose ends. Actually, I was quite sad about it for months; I went back to school and drank away my pain. I ended up hooking up with many boys as a distraction.

When I met Liam, I found him to be goofy and fun; I felt his awkwardness when he first started speaking with me. I did not pay attention; I was more focused on getting the gig over with. I hated having to wear a maid's uniform and being on my feet for eight to ten hours, serving overindulged and snobby guests who only cared about which designer people were wearing and what car they drove into the parking lot.

Liam continues, "So what do you think happened next?"

Sean and Patrick had no clue, so they looked at their grandfather with blank stares and then looked at each other. The older one said, "No idea," and shrugged his shoulders.

"Well, I worked it so that I would be standing next to Grace during cocktail hour. I gave this other server ten bucks to let me take his assignment. He welcomed the money and agreed to the deal. The event started, the line was forming, and I was standing right next to Grace. I was serving the beef Wellington, and she was serving the mini crab cakes. I said to her, 'Hi, I am Liam. Look at the line forming. This is going to be a long night.' Grace seemed to be distracted, looking at something down below the table. 'What are you looking at?' I asked her.

"'Oh, I always bring a book with me. I prop it out of the way, so the manager doesn't see it. There's always some downtime at these events. I'm Grace.'

"I was trying to keep the conversation going, so I asked her, 'Is this your first summer doing this work?'

"Grace replied, 'Yes, and absolutely my last. Catering is, without a doubt, not for me. I mean, look at these uniforms that we have to wear. And most of the work is on weekends. It is not much of a summer.'

"I was just mesmerized by Grace's eyes, a deep sky blue, and became distracted. 'Um, did you say you worked here last summer?' I could tell immediately that I got caught not paying attention. I saw her laugh.

"She said, 'No, were you not listening?'

"With a red face, I owned it. Making an excuse, I said, 'Yes, sorry, I am getting distracted by the line. I guess it's go time.'

"For the rest of the cocktail hour, not much was said. I could see her glancing at her book between a crab cake or two. There were times I was going to bring on the charm, but could not get any words out of my mouth. She smiled at me once or twice, but mainly kept to herself. She wasn't much of a talker.

"Then the manager asked her to head towards the ballroom because he was assigning her to some tables in the back right-hand corner. As for me, I was assigned the opposite, the front left. I was annoyed because this task was messing with my game here.

"Grace said, 'Bye, Liam.'

"And I said, 'Yeah, see ya, Grace.' And that was it for the rest of the night. I was busy busing tables and taking orders. She was nowhere in sight, probably doing the same thing with her tables.

"The night ended, and I was on the hunt. I needed to see if I could talk to her again. I was trying to gain some momentum here."

The youngest grandson interrupted, "Well, you didn't really make an effort when you were standing next to her. Seemed kind of lame on your part."

Liam's response was short, "Okay, enough of that talk. Let me continue my story. It was the end of the night, and I was walking back to my car when I saw her, book in hand and walking to her car. She seemed in a rush to get home. Who could blame her? The job totally sucked. You were on your feet all day. Then this other server went up to her and was giving Grace a hard time. Asking her to hang with them at this local park. He had a flask in his hand; it was filled with vodka. They were blocking her door, and she seemed to be quite frustrated by it.

"And that's when I figured out my in. I came to her rescue, but she could not know it. She seemed to really value being independent and not needing anyone. I jumped in and said, 'Where you guys going?' And I could see relief in Grace's face when she saw me. I don't even remember their names. They were kind of losers.

"One of the guys said, 'We are planning to go to park with this,' and he holds out the flask. 'We have more of it in the car. It's Saturday night. It's our time to party now.'

"I told him, 'Well, officially it's Sunday morning, but I get you. I am out; I'll catch up with you guys next Saturday. I'll be working this shit job again, serving some rich assholes. But it will help me with my slush fund for college. Grace, you ready to go?'

"Grace said, 'Definitely.'

"The two guys left; they were more about getting wasted than anything. Their departure left Grace and me alone. Finally, I was waiting for my shot.

"Grace looked at me and said, 'Hey, thanks. I thought those guys would never leave me alone. They are kind of—'

"I say, 'Losers.'

"Grace smiles and says, 'Exactly. I owe you one. Have a good night.'

"'I will hold you to that. Good night, Grace.'

"'Good night, Liam. See you later.'"

Sean and Patrick were wanting to know more. "So did you go out with her? Did you kiss her? What happened next?"

Liam chuckled and responded, "Okay, okay, boys, I am getting to that part. So after the car incident... Well, I saved her life—she said herself that she owed me."

As he said that, Sean rolled his eyes.

"Plus, girls always love that knight-in-shining-armor shit. Grace was different though; she was very independent. She didn't need anyone, although the situation got her attention. She did see me and wasn't distracted by any book. The next day at work, I approached her. I had a bit more swagger."

Patrick, with a confused look on his face, asked, "Swagger? What's that."

Liam snapped back with, "What are these schools teaching you? You don't know what that means? Okay, it's another word for confidence...or arrogance. In this case, let's go with confidence."

Patrick nodded.

Liam continued, "So the next day, I say, 'Hey, Grace, how's it going?'

"'It's okay, back here at work. Living the dream.'

"'Yeah, this job pretty much sucks, but it is my ticket out of this town. If I stay with this job, I am away to college in the fall. I am going to UNH.'

"Grace asks, 'Why does the job matter so much? You got in, so wouldn't you go anyway? Who cares about this gig?!'

"'Well, my parents do. Most jobs I stay about two weeks, so this time I have to show them that I can stay the summer, which is kinda hard. This kind of work is not for me.'

"'What? The jobs that deal with people?!'

"That is what I liked about Grace, her sarcasm. And she always had my number.

"'Yep, pretty much, Grace. But I will finish this job because I have to. I am excited about college and don't want to blow it.'

"Grace nodded and said, 'I get it.'

"'So you want to go out this Sunday night? I'm not working and didn't see you on the schedule. I'll even take you to dinner. I'm feeling generous these days, although it is not because of this job. The pay is shit for all the work we do.'

"Grace says, 'Can't debate that fact; my feet kill me after an event in this place. Yeah, I'll go.'

"'Okay, I'll pick you up at seven.'

"'Here's my address.' She handed me a piece of paper.

"'Thanks, see you then.'

"I decided to choose a restaurant that was a bit nicer. Deep down, I liked Grace more than the other girls. She was unique, and she kept me on my toes. She challenged me. I liked that. I knew I was out of my league with Grace, but that's why I was so drawn to her. So let's fast forward here. We went to dinner and had a great time. She opened up more, and surprisingly, I did as well. We were at dinner for hours, and then I drove her home. And gave her a respectable kiss, nothing over-the-top. By the end of the evening, I knew I was into her. Really into her."

Oh yes, that dinner, I remember that. That's when I saw him in a different light. He had some depth to him. He wasn't just talking about sports; he shared more about his hopes and dreams. That was one of my favorite first dates. I really started to like him after that dinner.

"Boys, it was my favorite summer. Grace and I hung out the entire summer. We would go to the beach, the park, grab a coffee—she introduced me to the Americano. She became my best friend in a whole four weeks, and at the time, I would do anything for her. But

I knew that both she and I were going away, and there was part of me that did not want to get attached. I knew I was going to college, and there would be plenty of girls, parties, and booze. I was not interested in starting my freshman year with a girlfriend. I didn't want to be tied down. I was thinking, *These will be the best four years of my life*. But I ignored that and kept seeing Grace and getting more and more attached.

"And then it happened. We had sex. I knew it was headed that way and wanted it badly. I didn't want it to change things, but I was not ready to be super serious and in a committed relationship."

As I said, Liam was my first. In that moment, I felt so connected and safe. I think we were both in love. I was glad I experienced it with Liam. I was glad I waited until I was in love. Some of my friends had sex prior to their senior year, which was fine, but I never felt inclined to sleep with anyone…well, until Liam came into my life.

We developed this bond over four weeks. I was seeing him almost every day. At the time, I felt bad because there were times that I was supposed to go out with Hope, but I found myself staying home with Liam. I was in love. I felt adored by him and enjoyed his company.

At the time, and even looking back now, it was strange to me. We were so incredibly different, but we just worked. It was hard for me to even understand. I knew he cared for me, even loved me. I could tell by the way he looked at me. His eyes said it all. I knew we were leaving for college, but I couldn't *not* be with him. I was already attached, and it was intoxicating. I never thought I was one of those girls who would be so smitten, but I was. And at the time, it felt so good.

But then I remember the awkward conversation as we were both headed in separate directions to go away for four years. A lot can happen in that pivotal time.

"Now, boys, I was in a bind. I really liked—truthfully, loved—this girl, but I was so conflicted. I imagined school as drinking, going to parties, playing hockey, and I guess studying too. My image of my college years was not leaving school every weekend to visit my girlfriend. No way. I wanted to fully embrace the college experience, like I'd seen it in the movies.

"I was the one who left for college first. Then Grace headed to her school a week later. It was awkward that last night. We talked about staying together, but deep down I was restless about it. I knew I loved Grace and did not want to lose her, but I knew my desire for freedom and fun were more important. This was my chance to let loose and go crazy. I knew having a girlfriend would put a damper on it.

"I agreed to stay in the relationship and have her as my girlfriend; I could tell she wanted that. We settled on it, but I wasn't sure how it would work. If I really thought about it, I didn't feel I was capable of making the commitment.

"We did mention getting together on Columbus Day weekend. It was only six weeks away. What could change during that time? I would just be getting used to school."

I remember that last night Liam is talking about. It was the night we said goodbye. We agreed to stay together, and that was the answer I wanted to hear. We were getting closer, and I did not want to lose that. But there was something about that night that was off. He was saying the right things, but something in my gut was not buying it. I was so unsettled when we parted. I even started to get a bit teary-eyed as we had our last kiss. It surprised both of us, I was not much of a crier, and he knew that. There was a pit in my stomach; I knew things were going to change, even as I told myself they wouldn't. I saw Liam get into his car and drive off into the sunset. The timing and the atmosphere seemed to be out of a book. It felt like he was leaving forever. For some reason, I found our conversation to be more of a "goodbye and good luck," rather than a "see you in a month or so." We had planned to get together for the long Columbus Day weekend, which was about six weeks away. That wasn't so long to be away from each other.

But then, in my first month of school, I was inspired to take action. Half because I was a bit homesick, and the other half because I really did miss him. The phone calls were okay, but usually they were cut short due to our packed schedules, meeting new friends, and getting acclimated to the workload. Although, I was more about diving into the curriculum than he was. I knew he hadn't stepped foot into the library yet. He may get there, maybe by the end of freshman year, but probably not before then. His focus was on the social scene.

I had an idea. Why not surprise him? I was going to school in New England as well; maybe I could see him one Friday night and stay for the weekend. I found out which dorm he was in and borrowed a car from a new friend I met during orientation week. She offered to come along with me, so that worked out smoothly. Additionally, Frank, one of Liam's high school friends went to UNH. I'd met him during the summer, so I was able to contact him to help me with logistics and the surprise.

There was a party at another dorm that night, so my new friend and I were to make an entrance. I remember being a bit nervous, because typically I didn't do things like that. For a split second I thought, *What if he doesn't want to see me?* It was a fleeting idea, because my energy was more aligned with the excitement of seeing Liam. The irony was that, when I got to the party, I was the one who was surprised.

♡

Exploration Questions
Chapter 11
Liam

1. Do you remember your first love? What did you learn from that experience?

2. How was your first encounter with sexual intercourse? What were your expectations? Were they met, or were you disappointed about the experience?

3. Who was the "one who got away" in your life?

4. Have you ever dated someone in whom at first you had no interest? If so, how did your feelings change along the way?

5. How has love evolved in your relationships? What is important now, as opposed to when you were younger?

Chapter 11 Activity

Write a Valentine to One of Your Great Loves: For this task, include everything you received from this love. Was this the one who introduced you to good wine or food? Did this love share or awaken your love of the outdoors or live music? Use this valentine to celebrate the wins, not the losses of this love. There's no need to send it unless you feel it would be for both parties' highest good. It is more about your acknowledging it for your own growth and development.

Chapter 12

Liam—Part 2

L iam asked Patrick, "Hey, can you grab me another blanket; it's getting colder in here."

I saw both Sean and Patrick exchange a look with each other. I sensed they knew their grandfather was on borrowed time.

"Sure, here you go." One of the boys threw a blanket on Liam's lap. "Better?"

"Yeah, thanks. Okay, so as I was saying, we decided to stay together, and I knew it may not be the best idea. But I did really love her and couldn't let her go when I left. The minute I left, my summer and my high school life was done. I moved on. Now I had this incredible opportunity to start over, a fresh start. It was time to ramp up the partying. And UNH was the perfect place to do it.

"The minute I unpacked and moved into my dorm, I was ready to meet new friends and, of course, check out the women. And I was happy to be away from my parents. I could do anything there; the freedom was intoxicating. So I did…everything. I went to a dorm party that first night and had a blast. And from that party on, I never looked back.

"The only problem was that I still had Grace. And I was so split; part of me wanted to end it, and the other part wanted her forever. Instead of dealing with it, I immersed myself in intramural hockey, a few classes, and parties. I wasn't even around for her calls. I would be somewhere, or I would only speak with her for a minute or two because I was running to something else. I made myself real busy.

Her not being around made me forget about this situation, even though my first thought when I woke up was Grace. She had made her mark on me."

Sean asked, "What did you do? Did you end up seeing her Columbus Day weekend?"

Liam responded, "Well, we never made it to that point."

Sean said, "Oh, really?!"

I remember buying a new outfit to wear for the surprise visit to Liam. I had butterflies the week prior to my trip to UNH. I was excited to see him because we really hadn't talked the past couple of weeks. He would call, and I would be in the middle of something; he was hard to connect with as well.

The timing never seemed to be right with us. I think that's what prompted me to go see him. I wanted to feel close to him again. I knew it had only been a couple of weeks, but I was already feeling that he was in my past and not part of my future. I didn't usually feel insecure, especially with Liam, but in that moment, I had to take action. I took matters into my own hands and drove up with my new friend Abbey, who graciously agreed to take the two-hour road trip up north with me.

It was time for my reunion with Liam. My hands were clammy, and my heart was racing for the entire drive. My friend played fun music, and we laughed and sang, which put me more at ease. However, once I arrived at the campus, all the nerves came back. I was so excited to see Liam; it seemed as if it had been so long since we'd seen each other, but in reality it had only been three weeks. I guess it was because I was used to seeing him almost every day during the summer. I got used to that cadence and really enjoyed our time together. It was a unique experience for me. I usually did not fall for guys, but something about Liam impacted me in an unusual way. It was good…and terrifying at the same time.

Our plan was to meet Liam's friend Frank, a cool guy who was very down-to-earth and always nice to me. He told me to meet him at the university library, which is in the Dimond Building. We knew that Liam wouldn't be there on Friday night, so it was a safe place to meet. Frank would then take me to the off-campus party where I would surprise Liam. I also thought that Frank may get along with my new friend Abbey. They both had a similar vibe, easygoing and fun.

We made it to the library and found Frank. I said, "Do you think he suspects anything? I have done my best to not talk real long with him. I did not want to ruin the surprise."

Frank replied, "He has no clue. But let's face it; Liam is a bit clueless about things. He doesn't always catch on."

I said, "Okay, let's go. And by the way, this is Abbey, my new friend from Providence College."

Abbey said, "Hi, Frank."

Frank responded with a smile and said, "Nice to meet you. So you ladies ready? Let's get some drinks."

Frank took us to this house not far from campus. It had four flights of stairs, and the hallways smelled like stale beer and cigarettes. I was thinking, *This place is nasty, so gross.* It was the epitome of a college apartment building. Many floors and several apartments crammed into one house. You could hear diverse types of music coming from each door. Of course, the apartment where the party was being held was on the fourth floor. The stairs were brutal, and I was thinking, *This better be worth it.*

Frank went in first, and then Abbey followed. I was the last to go through the doorway. Music was blasting, and it was very crowded. Clouds of smoke permeated every room. The kitchen was small, just enough room for a small table and a keg of beer. The floor was a bit sticky as I walked around, looking for Liam. I was hoping I'd find him.

Then there he was. I recognized his favorite navy-blue hoodie he wore everywhere. He wasn't alone. He was in a back corner with another girl. I saw him embracing and kissing her. My heart dropped in my chest, and I couldn't breathe for a couple of seconds, which at the time felt like an eternity.

What is happening here? My mind was racing with millions of questions. *Didn't we agree to stay together? Did we talk about seeing other people? How can he have forgotten about me in three weeks? How could he do this to me? To us? Didn't we have something special?*

Frank and Abbey looked shell-shocked. I could see by the look on his face that Frank regretted helping me coordinate the surprise. They kept turning their heads from me to Liam, and back again.

Liam was in his own world for a few minutes, and then he sensed that something was happening. He looked up and inadvertently stared directly into my eyes. Liam saw my surprise and then sadness as I gaped at him.

I had no words. I felt paralyzed; all I could do was just stand there and look at him.

Then I heard the girl he was hooking up with say to him, "Who's that? Do you know her?"

Liam responded, "Grace."

When he said my name, it prompted me to leave immediately. I had to go. I couldn't deal with what was happening. I didn't want to hear his explanation or rationalization. This was a time that he could not escape his behavior. His charm would not pull him through this one. I ran down four flights of stairs and got to the bottom, winded and devastated. I thought, *Now what am I going to do?*

I was followed by Abbey. And when she saw me, she gave me a hug and said, "Let's get the hell out of here and get something to eat." We ran to her car and drove back to Providence College. I didn't want to stay on Liam's campus a minute longer.

Abbey and I remained friends for the rest of my time on Earth. When a friend has your back like that, you keep them for good. I will always appreciate Abbey's being there for me. I never forgot, even now in the afterlife.

Sean said, "How could that be? I thought you were crazy about this girl. How could you blow it in a few weeks?"

Liam chuckled. "Well your grandpa had a way of screwing up things, especially when he was young. Luckily, I got a bit smarter when I met your nana. Plus, your nana always had the knack for keeping me in line. Okay, so let me explain what happened here.

"So the first three weeks of school were epic. I loved it the minute I walked on campus. I owned the place. There was so much fun all around me. I didn't even have to wait for the weekend. I could grab a beer on a Tuesday night at the dive bar right off campus. I got one of those fake IDs in the first week. But don't tell your mother that I did that. She would be mad at me for that. Once I had that ID, the sky was the limit! I loved all the freshman events; it was a chance to check out the talent and meet some kindred spirits. Everyone was ready to meet new friends and go out. There were times in the first couple of weeks that I skipped a few classes. I could make it up and figure it out later. My priority was to be where I could have the most fun, even if I did not know anyone. I'd make friends. You know how charming I can be."

I saw both grandsons roll their eyes, and in unison they say, "Yeah, Grandpa, we know."

"It was Friday night, and it was such a fun party. I started talking to this pretty girl. I couldn't believe it because, truthfully, going on looks alone, she was way out of my league. We started talking hockey, and she definitely knew her stuff. It made me even more attractive to this random girl. After four beers, I found myself kissing her on the chair in the corner of the room. The music, the booze, and my...you know." Liam looks at his crotch.

"And then, as I look up—I am not sure how long I was making out with this girl—I see Grace standing there. And at first, it doesn't make sense. *What the hell is Grace doing here?* Her blue eyes are boring into me with disbelief and then sadness. I knew in that moment that I'd really hurt Grace. Even with the booze in my system, the buzz completely went away once I locked eyes with her. She did not even say anything. It would have been better if she'd yelled at me, or even hit me. Grace did not. I said her name and then watched her sprint down the stairs. I didn't even get to explain or say anything. I was stunned. I kept wondering, *What is she doing here? Did I make plans with her this weekend? How could I have done this to her? I am an asshole. A total douchebag.*

"Then I see my buddy Frank. He shrugs his shoulders and says to me, 'I thought you would appreciate the surprise. I didn't know this would happen. Sorry, man.'

"I responded, 'What? What just happened here? Did you know she was coming?'

"Frank said, 'Yeah. I coordinated it with Grace. She wanted to surprise you. It seems that she is the one that was surprised.'

"'Do you know where she went? I got to find her.'

"'No clue, man. You are on your own with this one.'

"And that was it. I found out that Grace drove back to Providence College that night. I tried calling her all night and couldn't reach her. I almost even borrowed a friend's car the next day to explain and apologize. But I couldn't bring myself to do it. I felt a lot of shame. I didn't know what to say, except for, 'Yes, Grace, I am an ass, and you can totally do better,' which I left on her voice mail in her dorm. I didn't have the guts to say that I was in touch with how much of a coward I really was. I acted tough, but deep down I was a pussy. Oh, I shouldn't be using that word. I was a wimp.

"A week went by, and I finally got ahold of Grace on the phone. She was cold and wanted nothing to do with me. It was a ten-minute conversation, tops, and she let me know that it was best to break up for good. She had her new life, and I had mine. Realistically, it would never work; I couldn't keep the commitment. She realized that once she saw me. It was a sign for her to embrace college life and meet guys on her own campus.

"She was right, and I probably knew that deep down when we said goodbye. She was special, and at the time I couldn't let her go. That was it. I saw her once at a local bar one summer, and we did not say much. Grace had changed; she seemed more mature. As for me, I was the same ass…just a year or two older.

"I never forgot her. Looking back, she made such a difference in my life. I grew a lot when I was with her, even if it was just being with her for a summer. Grace was my first love, and I always regretted how I treated her in the end. I share this with you boys because true love is special. And if you find that girl, don't piss it away on some random hookup. You both will be in college shortly; have as much fun as you can. But, remember, if you find someone special, fight for her and cherish her."

Patrick asked, "What ever happened to Grace; did she ever get married, have a family?"

Liam said, "Well, no. She died pretty early in life, in her forties. She was hit by a car, pretty tragic. I never went to the funeral. I did not learn about her death until weeks after it happened. I even called her best friend from high school, Hope. I had met Hope a couple of times that summer. She told me what happened. She was a kind soul and said that I really meant a lot to Grace. And that was it. I never spoke a word about it again. Until now."

Patrick responded, "Grandpa, I didn't know you could be so deep. I can tell you really loved this girl."

Liam said, "And that is why I turned it around when I met your grandmother. I knew she was a good thing, and I didn't want to blow it again. Luckily, I learned my lesson the first time.

"Well, I know it is getting late, and your mom is going to pick you up in a few minutes. Thanks for coming by. I love you both very much.

You are my pride and joy. Always remember that." He hugged each one and said goodbye.

They both left knowing that they had just shared a special moment with their grandpa. He had told them a story they would not forget and had taught them a lesson they would keep in their hearts.

As I hear the story, I am so incredibly moved by Liam's version. I never knew how much I meant to him. At the time, I was devastated, but I'd rallied pretty quickly with all the fun distractions from school. Looking back, it was best for us to break up. The relationship would have stifled us. Maybe I was able to compartmentalize and just forget about it. Probably wasn't the healthiest way to cope.

Enzo arrives on the scene. "Well, hello, Enzo, fancy meeting you here." I've gotten used to him just popping in and out, so now I joke about it. "What brings you here? Good news for me?" I know he is going to give me some job to do.

Enzo grins. "Grace, you are looking well and full of light."

I think to myself, *He is such a wiseass, but truthfully, it is what I love about him. He challenges me and helps me to rise—no pun intended—to the occasion.* "What's up, E?"

He looks at me with a perplexed look.

"Enzo, I am assuming you are here for a reason."

"Yep. You are right on the money, Grace. You are getting good at this stuff. There's a reason you are here at this moment with Liam. Can you guess why?"

It takes me a minute, and suddenly all the pieces fall into place. Liam was reminiscing, he was giving his grandsons loving advice, and he looked frail, not well at all. "Liam is going to die, isn't he?"

Enzo responds, "Yes, that's right, Grace. Time's up for him."

"Oh, I guess it is. Does he know it?"

"He has a sense. That's why he asked to see his grandsons one last time. It was a goodbye for him."

"Okay, so how am I involved in this? I heard him tell the story about us. I never thought about it from his perspective. It was very healing for me to hear how much I meant to him. At the time, I was so devastated when I found him kissing someone else. Somehow, I never held on to the anger or hurt. Or maybe I buried it. A month or two later, I was able to let go and move on. I had a blast in college; I do think that if we'd stayed together, I wouldn't have really fully experienced college. He would have been always there in the back of my head.

"It is interesting that he's held on to this for all these years. From my perspective, he doesn't need to do that anymore. I don't have any malice or anger towards him. He opened me up in a way that I never experienced before. Sure, we were young, but still, that experience with him really shaped me. So what's next, Enzo?"

"Well, you are going to help him cross over."

"Really, how do I do that? I haven't even fully crossed over. I've been in limbo for I don't know how long."

"You'll figure it out, Grace. I have faith in you."

"Okay."

Suddenly I appear right in front of Liam. His eyes widen, and he says, "Grace, is that you? It can't be you. No way. I have not seen you in forever. You look the same. How is this possible?! Am I losing it here?"

"Hi, Liam. Yes, it is me, Gracey. Remember? You used to call me that. I only let certain people call me that."

"Yes, your grandfather called you that, and you loved him very much. And I think your best friend in high school called you that. What was his name? Well, I can't remember much these days. See how old I am."

I smiled at him. "Yes, physically you look a bit different. But emotionally, you still seem like that eighteen-year-old."

Liam laughed. "Yeah, you always had my number. And called me out on my shit. That is the reason I fell in love with you."

Using my quick wit, I quipped, "That's the main reason? I thought it was my winning personality."

"Well, that too. And you were really smart and had beautiful eyes. Actually, the list could go on and on.

"Are you dead? What is really happening here? Or am I delusional? They have me on all these pain pills. I could be hallucinating. This, I would have enjoyed in my college days. Not so much now."

"The good news is that I can tell you that you are not losing it. I am actually here in spirit and soul. I've been doing some reflection since I died. It is kind of a long story. If you can believe it, I've even been with a spirit guide, and his name is Enzo. Back to my Italian roots and connected with a fellow paesano. Go figure. And seeing you is not as much about me as it is about you. I feel like you have to talk to me. So what's up?"

"I was very sad when you died many years ago. I never got to say goodbye and to say I was sorry for what I did. I usually never have regrets, but with you it was different. That way I treated you was one of my biggest regrets. And I am really sorry, Grace. I loved you, but I was not in the right headspace to be in a committed relationship. It is no excuse, but it is the truth. I had to go a little crazy and enjoy life. I always wished we had met later in life, when I had my shit together. But we didn't, and I fucked things up, so that was that."

"Liam, what I've learned recently is that people come in and out of our lives. It may be for a season or a lifetime. Each relationship we learn from and have the opportunity to expand from at a soul level. We don't see it that way on Earth. We are so blind; we don't always learn and grow from it. And then we move on to the next and sometimes take our baggage from past relationships to the future ones. A lot of it is unconscious behavior; we don't even realize we are doing it.

"Since I died, I've been provided a new perspective on how people come into our lives for a reason. We don' know it at the time, but I feel it is all about us being closer to love. Embracing and learning how to love fully, not only others, but also ourselves."

Liam smiled. "This death stuff has made you a bit deep. What happened to Gracey, the bookworm who lived in her head? You didn't express many feelings when we were together."

I laughed and then responded, "She's still part of me, but now I've been able to focus on the other aspects of me. The ability to receive, be open to love, really feel experiences, and trust. The transformation is not about others, but about me, my soul's journey."

I was surprised at how easily this was all coming to me. Enzo was right; I knew what to say and do.

"So what now, Gracey?"

I paused and wanted to give Liam the opportunity to figure it out on his own. He did.

"It's time for me to go, isn't it, Grace?"

"Yes, Liam, it is time. I want you to know how special you were to me. You were my first love. And I always remembered you in a loving way once I got past the incident. I forgave you a long time ago. Now it is your turn to forgive...you."

"Okay"—he paused, I saw a heaviness lift from his shoulders, and then his eyes filled up—"I will. Where do we go from here? What's next?"

"There's someone here to greet you."

At that moment, I made space for Liam's wife. It was her job to officially cross him over and usher him into the light. I was there to help heal him and hand him off to his wife. Once I saw her take his hand, I knew my task was over.

I could see the joy in Liam's eyes when he saw his wife. He was always meant to be with her, not with me. I helped him to be more open to love, and he helped me. And I will always love him deep in my soul for that; I'm incredibly grateful for Liam.

♡

Exploration Questions
Chapter 12
Liam—Part 2

1. Were you ever brave enough to get your heart broken? If yes, why? If no, why not?

2. What would be the benefit of having others forgive you and of your forgiving others?

3. After one heartbreaking experience, what made you get out there to try again?

4. Have you ever been present when a loved one crossed over?

5. How has that impacted you?

Chapter 12 Activity

Say Goodbye and Forgive with Love. Who are 3 people by whom you were hurt in your life? For each person, say how they hurt you and how you can forgive them. They tried their best; wish them well. Say 5 times, "I forgive you, _(name here)__."

Chapter 13

Debrief

I look around. I am not in our usual spot in Central Park. This is another favorite neighborhood of mine—well, maybe it lost some of its shine when I got hit by a car here. That moment definitely put a damper on my feelings for this spot. Now, being on West Fourteenth Street, I am standing with a sea of cobblestones at my feet. The Meatpacking District was one of my favorites when I lived here. There were a lot of tourists from time to time, which could be extremely annoying, but that did not take away my appreciation for the fancy boutiques, trendy restaurants, and stretch of the High Line, an elevated park built atop former railroad tracks.

There's no one here. It's dead. The bright spot is where I died and where I met Enzo. I remember how stunning I looked that day. What a waste! At least, I looked good at the breakup. I know I did because of the look on Derrick's face.

Oh, I wonder how he is doing now. I am over it. We were not right together. Our fundamental values were so different. He was angry at the world and wanted everyone to give to him. Me? I enjoyed working for everything I had. It gave me a sense of purpose.

I wonder what I'm doing here.

"Hey, Grace. Remember this spot?" says Enzo

"Oh yes. Our first meeting."

"That's right."

"And where I died. Minor detail. Why are we here?"

"Keep you guessin'," he says and winks at me. "It's where you started."

"Feels like a long time ago."

"You went through a lot. You should be proud."

"I guess I did. I learned much more about myself. I can't believe that I could be that introspective."

"What's the chance of that, Grace?" Again, Enzo giving me a hard time.

I do love that about him. I am feeling a bit sad because it seems that we are coming to a close. I will miss him.

Enzo says, "I've set up a movie screen here. Let's go back to see what's happened. And here's your favorite." He hands me a big white cup of warm goodness. "I made this a bit differently. Try it."

I taste it and feel the fluffy cloud of dairy foam. It's whipped cream and some cinnamon. "Wow, this is fantastic. Cappuccino?"

"Yeah, that's more of a treat than an Americano. No?"

"True. You know your beverages, Enzo." I smile as I give him the compliment.

We sit down in comfy La-Z-Boy rocking chairs, the ones in which you can lean back and instantly get in a relaxed zone. And, of course, on its side is a cupholder for my delicious cappuccino. Or maybe, for this movie, the appropriate beverage is a glass of wine. Not that I am complaining. Suddenly, a huge movie screen appears. *How does he do this? He is connected.*

"Grace, let's take a look."

An old-fashioned projector starts whirring, and the 5...4...3...2...1 countdown begins on the screen. Just like an old movie. The movie opens with Grayson and Amy seated in a restaurant. They are at a two-top, slurping spaghetti and talking animatedly. It reminds me of the scene from the Disney movie *Lady and the Tramp*. They are looking into each other's eyes and very present with one another. And there isn't a cell phone visible anywhere. *Wow, that is a miracle!*

Grayson stops talking and listens intently to Amy. As Amy tells a story, Grayson is smiling as she is talking. He has not looked at his phone once. *Good job, Grayson.* Amy is laughing, and her eyes are twinkling. She gets up in the middle of the dinner to go to the ladies' room, and she twirls around in her sexy, beautiful cocktail dress. Her hair bounces as she gets up. She definitely got a blowout.

Grayson looks handsome. His shirt is pressed nicely, not one wrinkle. He is wearing black slacks, and even his shoes are shined. Grayson has definitely stepped up his game. When Amy comes back to the table, he reaches across and places his hand on top of Amy's. He says, "Let's get dessert. We still have plenty of time before the babysitter needs to leave."

Amy responds, "I love that idea."

Even the other tables can feel their connection. One woman is jealous of the intimacy; she thinks to herself, *I wish I had that with my husband.*

Enzo says, "See that?"

I respond, "I do. Amazing."

"You really helped Grayson see aspects of himself that he needed to change in order to make his marriage work. Since you spent time with him, he's quit his job and found one where he can leave at a normal time. He's home for dinner, instead of coming home at 8:00 p.m. when the kids are already in bed. He plans at least two dates a month with Amy. He's learned that her happiness is a priority, which in turn has made him proud and happy with himself."

"Wow. I am so proud of him."

"Grace, how about you? What did you learn?"

"It was both of us. It was not just him or just me. I blamed him for all our problems. I made it all about his being a workaholic. His lack of presence and his working a lot made me feel that I was not enough for him. And there is no doubt that it was a factor, but it was not all his fault.

"I was so shut down. I put up such a wall when it came to my own needs. I was embarrassed by them. I never had the courage to express what I needed because I felt it would turn him off. I did not honor my needs. I was not taking care of myself. By not sharing, it backfired. I held in my needs until I exploded because I did not express them sooner. I stewed over situations, conversations, slights. And it would build and build, and then explode because I was not voicing what I needed. I was fiercely independent; I felt expressing my needs was a sign of weakness.

"Because I did not acknowledge my needs, others could not honor them either. How could they if I didn't communicate them? Likewise, I realized that Grayson had his own insecurities and was just doing what he needed to do. I see that he was there to challenge my thinking. When I was alive, I never really learned the lesson. I just went on to the next relationship.

"I have learned how important it is to advocate for yourself."

Enzo asked, "What would you do differently if you were to do it all over again?"

"Well, I would express my feelings more. I would take the risk and be real with people close to me. I didn't share with Grayson because maybe, deep down, I thought he couldn't handle it or would reject me. The thing is, we broke up anyway."

"From the looks of it, he learned a lot from you as well. Mission accomplished for both of you."

I look back at the screen and now see Matty, my best guy friend, playing fetch with his black lab, Cody. He is running around with joy in his step. He is being goofy and talking to the dog. The dog is having fun and running from place to place.

Matty always loved dogs and wanted a Lab all his life. His parents were never in favor of getting a dog. They did not want to have to take care of it. The minute he got married, he got a dog, even before he bought a home. Cody is his second dog, and he's made more time to play with him on weekends.

His face looks the same, and his hair has the salt-and-pepper look. He seems the same, but even more joyful. This makes me smile inside.

Enzo asked, "What about this one?"

"By going back to that time, I remembered how Matty and I had such a good time together. Memories that I had forgotten about over the years. He was my best friend in ways, different than with Hope. I never realized what an impact I had on him, and he on me. I learned so much, going back to that time and witnessing what happened. He was such a kind soul. He really loved me for me. I am glad that I got to see him and to be there. I am hoping that it helped him heal or look at the situation a little bit differently."

"Do you think it was just bad timing that kept you from dating each other?"

"Not sure. I did the best I could with that situation. I couldn't receive his love at the time; for some reason, I could not see him in a romantic way. I couldn't make the shift to boyfriend and girlfriend. I just couldn't. It was not him; it was me. It was not even something I was conscious of, but I couldn't accept it. I felt, deep down, he really saw me and adored me. For me, I enjoyed being with him and could really be myself. That was not something I could often do with boys or guys."

Enzo said, "It was a reminder that there were men in your life who adored you. They were there, even though you could not always see them."

"True, I didn't really see it at the time. Yet I did feel bad about what happened. I knew I hurt him. I just hope that I rectified that when I went back and was there when he felt rejected."

"Yep, he moved on after that. Ya know, guys will be guys."

"Well, okay, Enzo."

"Hey, guys have needs. They can't wait around forever."

"Okay, I got it Enzo. Loud and clear. What's the next scene?"

Then the picture shows Hope and her family. It is a beautiful day; the sun is shining bright. They are in a soccer field, where there are bleachers in front of a stage and podium. Most people are all dressed up in various styles of suits and dresses; although, there is an occasional person in jeans. Hope is wearing a bohemian, flowing dress covered in blues, purples, and pinks. She has really aged well. Hope looks happy. Very proud. And I see a sea of black caps approaching. There's a lot of energy and excitement. It is high school graduation.

Oh, it must be Gracey's. "Enzo, are they celebrating Gracey's graduation from high school? Is that what I am witnessing here?"

"You are quick. Did the cap and gown give it away?" he jokes.

I've learned to adore Enzo's sarcasm. "Pretty much, Enzo. It was you who said I was smart and quick-witted. Right?!"

"Yep, I did say that."

"Oh my God. She's so big. She's a young adult, looks like her mom. She's beautiful."

"Hope is one proud mama and still with her guy. Thanks to you."

"I have my besties back foreva. Even death could not separate us. She knew that, I think. Right?"

"Do I need to really answer that?"

"No, I got the answer. I knew it when I left her in Central Park. She felt me. I was there for her."

"Okay, that's the movie. The end."

"That was fast."

"Those were some of the final highlights. I am a man of few words, or I guess a guide of few words. Gotta go. See ya later."

And—poof!—once again, he disappears suddenly. Not sure why I am always surprised by that. It is his MO.

I then find myself on a park bench right near the Reservoir. I am sitting next to a man; he's wearing black-knit hat and workout clothes, and is all sweaty.

Wait a minute! Is this Derrick? Oh my God, this has come full circle. I guess this is part of the plan.

I sit there and just listen. He can't see or feel me, of course. I guess he is not supposed to; otherwise, he would know I was right beside him.

"Grace, I just went for a run. We used to do this together. I guess this is why I am talking to you out loud. Or I could just be going crazy? Anyway, you always beat me. I kind of hated you for that. You were always in better shape than I was. You never said anything or rubbed it in my face, but we both knew. Ever since I heard you died, I've been coming here every week. There's a part of me that feels a bit responsible for your death. Yeah, I know that I was not with you physically, but maybe you were distracted by the entire breakup. I don't know."

Runners fly by his bench, bringing him back to the present moment. He needs to run more; that helps him release his demons and get more grounded. Because of that, he needed this outlet maybe more than I did.

"I never did deserve you. In the end, that got really clear for me. And you knew it too. But you still loved me, with all my dysfunction. I knew, in the end, I could not be the man you deserved. I just couldn't. But it is not my fault. I had a messed-up childhood, and it made me broken. My dad was never there, and I felt lost. He worked all the time and was absent. And where's the support for me? What about me? Let's face it; everyone liked you better than me."

I hear this and no longer am provoked by his words. I actually feel bad for him. He's a pretty sad soul. He doesn't get it. There's such a lack of awareness of his impact on people and, more importantly, on himself.

He continues, "It is a year later, and you come into my mind quite a bit. I know I blew it, but you had your moments as well, Grace. I think you are right; I should go and see a therapist. But it is a lot of money, and I hate talking to strangers. I tried it once, and I am not sure it even did anything. I am going to probably end up alone. I think I am okay with that. It is easier. I do miss you; I know you gave me a lot, and looking back, I should have been grateful. But we did have some good times. Right, Grace? It wasn't all bad."

I reflect on his question and think there were definitely good times in the beginning, but in the end, it was a train wreck. Time has gone by, but he is the same. Maybe a little more awareness, but still clueless about his impact on me. At least one of us has learned from the experience. *Oh well, some people are not capable of change. And that is a harsh reality that most people face.*

As Derrick's talking, I drown him out with my own thoughts. *Does it matter now? I need to forgive myself.* In my gut, I knew he was not healthy, and I just stayed. For months. I so badly wanted it to work. I had pictured it all in my mind. Moving into a beautiful apartment. Walking down the aisle at our wedding in a winery—it sounds crazy, but I had it pictured that way in my mind—as Derrick gazes at me with love. And so many other memories I created. None of them happened. It was an illusion. A figment of my imagination.

I get out of my head and start paying attention to him again. "Grace, I am sorry if I somehow caused your death. I don't know where you are. You know me; I was never religious, never believed in the afterlife. We die, and life is over. That's it. There are no ghosts or spirits. But here I am, speaking to you. What is wrong with me? So prove me wrong. If you can hear me, give me a sign. A sign that you are listening."

Suddenly, Derrick is on his knees with his hands clasped together. The behavior is unlike him. He wasn't religious, but maybe now he is at least open to believing in a higher power. To believing that there is more to life than just the physical world. If he were able to have a connection with God, it would do him some good.

Okay, what can I do for a sign? All of a sudden, I wave my arms and have the power to create a gust of wind right next to him. Not sure how I was able to make that happen. Leaves and twigs suddenly fill the air. It gains his attention.

He is a bit confused. It causes him to go back to the bench and sit down. He doesn't want all of Central Park to think he's crazy.

And then a guy greets him, "Hey, man. Did you see a girl wandering around here, maybe looking for someone? I was supposed to meet this girl on a date, and it is looking like she stood me up."

"Yeah, did you meet her through an app?"

"How did you know?"

"Well, she was a no-show. It is a bit early for a date, isn't it?" asks Derrick.

"It was her idea; she likes to meditate in the park in the morning."

"Oh, one of those chicks."

"Well, she had some hot pics. The yoga-pants ones are my favorite. Anyways, I had an extra coffee. Do you want it? Don't want it to go to waste."

"Why don't you drink a second cup?"

"It's an Americano. Not a big fan. I am more of a latte guy."

"Sure, I'll take it. Thanks. I knew a girl that loved these. Thanks again, man. I got my sign."

The guy had a goofy look on his face. "Sign?"

"Never mind. Don't worry about it."

"Yep, enjoy." The stranger walked away.

Derrick says, "Got it, Grace. You know I am not much into the woo-woo shit, but this was very clear. Thanks, and I really am sorry. And hope you are okay, no matter where you are."

I got my sign as well. Got it loud and clear—he won't change. He may die alone and never have a lasting relationship, but that's not my concern. It's his journey, and he has the free will to live his life the way he desires. What I need to do is let it go, forgive him, and wish him well.

Additionally, forgive myself for staying in an unhealthy relationship and betraying myself when I knew I needed to get out six months earlier than I did. I say to myself, *Grace, don't look back in anger. You did your best, and that was his best.* I am letting this go now for good.

I start to see a very bright light sparkling through the trees. It is the most beautiful energy. It's mesmerizing; the powerful force is drawing me in. I left Derrick and started to walk along the Reservoir, following it naturally.

The light becomes brighter and brighter. I am guessing that this is *the* light. *But wait! Where's Enzo? He usually pops up around now. That's weird. Shouldn't he be here in this moment? Is it my graduation time?* I am torn since I am so drawn to the light, every piece of me knows I need to move forward and head right towards it.

I have to say goodbye to Enzo. It wouldn't be like him to not see me off. I stop in my tracks and delay. I know I need to go, but my heart wants to see Enzo. Thank him for all his grace and patience with my healing. Enzo did hook me up with some Americanos and even a cappuccino along this journey.

"Enzo, Enzo, where are you?" I knew in my gut he would come, so I wait. It seemed like an eternity, but it technically was about eleven Earth seconds.

"You called…and here I am, gracing you with my presence. Get it? Gracing you." And all of a sudden, he belts out a deep belly laugh. His voice is always a bit raspy and gritty.

I laugh and am so happy to see him that I don't even make fun of his corny joke.

"No sarcastic comment from you? Boy, you must have healed from this process." He winks, and his face lights up with a warm, playful smile.

"I guess so. You healed me." And I wink back with my own smile.

"No, not me. It was all you. Ain't gonna take credit for your work."

"Yeah, I know. It's not your style."

"This is the part where you are supposed to share all your learning. I'd like this to be brief. Narrow it down to the highlights. I like things to the point."

I say, "Let's start with this; some people never get it. They make the same mistakes and don't learn."

"Yeah, he's an ass. But you let it go, forgave him, and, most importantly, forgave yourself for staying in an unhealthy relationship."

I smile. "Yes, I did. And now I have peace. A grace—pun intended— that comes from within. It is about owning all of you. All the parts that make up who you are. Your gifts, strengths, dysfunction, and deep wounds. You don't need to wait until your life is over. Learning happens in our daily existence here on Earth. Life is now, and healing can start when you want it to happen. It is a choice over which you have more control than you think. What part within you needs healing? What do you need to express? What fear can you confront? And what can you let go of in life? This journey looks different for everyone. It is about being brave in your physical life, right here and right now. I learned that you need to be an advocate for yourself. I am enough. Express your needs. Love is infinite.

"Enzo, I don't think I could have gotten through this journey without your support and guidance. And the caffeine! I am incredibly grateful for you."

"I know. I'm your favorite guide. And the best-looking one you will see in the afterlife."

"That's for sure."

"Now go on before I go all soft on you. Keep heading towards the light. But before you step into the light, one more person wants to see you."

♡

Exploration Questions
Chapter 13
Debrief

1. What do you think Grace learned by revisiting her past relationships?

2. What have you learned about yourself in your current and past relationships?

3. As a result of the learning, what will you do differently?

4. What do you need to bring to the light and confront in your life?

5. What needs to happen to change the course of your relationships?

Chapter 13 Activity

Let Go of Limiting Beliefs: Write 3 limiting beliefs on 3 separate pieces of paper. Then take each limiting belief, and burn the paper. Make sure you do it in a place that is safe. Before burning it, rewrite the limiting belief on a new index card, making it into something more positive in nature, something that shows the possibility for change and growth.

Limiting belief: "I am never using a dating app again."

Honest and empowering belief: "I am right now taking a break from using the dating app and will check in a few months to see if I am up to trying it again."

OR

Limiting belief: "I am not lovable."

Honest and empowering belief: "Even though I am not in a relationship, I am open to being kind and loving myself during this time."

Chapter 14

New Beginnings

The light is still ever so present. As Enzo is saying that someone is waiting to see me, I notice a little boy in the distance, walking toward me through the trees. I can't seem to recognize him until he approaches the dirt path of the Reservoir. Now I do. I know that adorable face, those big brown eyes.

This is exactly how I remember him. My first love. Max. I can't believe he's right here, in front of me.

Enzo says, "Recognize this kid?"

"I do. He is still so adorable. Just like I remember."

"That's what happens. We bring the person back how you remember him."

"I lost touch with him when I moved. Did he die already?"

"Yeah, he got caught up in the wrong crowd. Died in his twenties. Overdose. Accidental. Shame. Strived for the popularity."

"That makes me sad. He was such an innocent kid. But he was easily swayed to do whatever it took to fit in."

Enzo sternly responds, "But we are not here to talk about his path. Max is here for you, Grace."

"He is?" I don't understand; I'm a bit confused.

"He knew that he was not nice to you when he was a little boy. He knew how much you liked him, and he took advantage of that. When we die, we get a snapshot of how we lived our lives. He knew deep down that he really hurt you and now sees the impact of his actions. He felt remorse during his post-life review. As souls, we always have an opportunity to do better. He wants to do better in the afterlife." Enzo steps aside and lets us have our moment.

Max is now right in front of me. I feel his love and light. It embodies him. Since he's eight years old in this moment, I kneel down to be at his level. I then look into his eyes; his innocence and virtue take me back and connect me with my inner child. I see myself in his eyes as a little girl, dancing and twirling around. I don't have a care in the world. There are no words to describe it; our souls are in sync. Bonded for eternity. It is almost as if we were one, simpatici. It is a healing energy I had never felt before.

Max reaches out, and I put my hand in his. He holds my hand softly and leads me closer to the light. I realize he's the soul who will help guide me into the light. I embrace Max and thank him for being here. We hug for a minute. No further words are uttered. There's only silence and healing.

After the hug, he acknowledges the moment by smiling. Max then disappears into the light; in a flash, he's gone.

And Enzo is back. "You made it. You graduated. You did so good I may even recommend you be a guide or something."

"Really?"

"Yeah, why not? If I can do this job, you sure as shit can do it. Great, here I go again. I'm still swearing. I'm still messin' up and learning myself. See that crowd of people? They're waiting for you. Go. Go. Go and greet them. They have been waiting here to welcome you to heaven. They all love you. These are people that have been in your life for centuries and who care for you and love you."

The energy is so beautiful. I know it is time. My time. My heart is filled with peace and grace. Before I take a step, I reach out and hug Enzo. I am not even sure it is allowed to hug a guide, but in that moment, I am not overthinking anything. I am moved to do it by my love for him and my gratitude.

Enzo hugs me back. "Yeah, yeah, I love you too. Now go on. It's time. I can't have you be late or have them wait any longer."

"Okay, I'm going."

This wave of light and love envelops me, and suddenly I see my grandpop, my nonno. He is standing there and beaming with light and love. I know he's been waiting for me. I am stepping into my new journey. And now I know I am home. I am home.

♡

Exploration Questions
Chapter 14

New Beginnings

1. What must you let go of in order to heal and move forward?
2. For what do you need to forgive yourself in your relationships?
3. How can you love yourself more every day?
4. What are you grateful for in your life?
5. How do you, or will you, find your grace within?

Chapter 14 Activity

Write a Positive Prayer or Intention: Using your own words, write a prayer or intention that states how you are firmly and powerfully learning and growing in love. There are limitless possibilities for expanding and transforming into a loving human being. Additionally, share the ways that love is showing up in your life. Flex your gratitude muscle!

Once it is written, read the prayer daily. Keep it alive by vocalizing gratitude for everything in your life that you enjoy and appreciate. Including YOU!

Acknowledgments

Danny and Annie—For your faith in me and ongoing enthusiasm as I wrote and published this book.

Nativa—My learning and growth motivated me to write this book. Thank you for the love and support to be ME.

Uncle Ray—Your creative spirit always inspires me.

Maggie—For encouraging me to own being a writer. Your coaching helped me tap into my creativity along the way.

Vivian, Karen, and Linley—For editing my articles and advocating for me to write.

PC Besties: Kristy, Cathy, and Emily—For always listening and being champions for my dreams.

Boys and Men in My Life—Thank you for contributing to my learning journey.

Index of Chapter Questions and Activity

Chapter 1 Questions- Grace

1. When do you know it is time to end a relationship? Do you initiate it or does your partner?

2. If you had the opportunity for a breakup do-over, what would you say or do differently during that discussion?

3. If you could see one ex again, who would it be, and what would you need to say to, or hear from, them for closure?

4. Have you ever stayed too long in a relationship? If so, what prevented you from getting out earlier?

5. How do you listen to your gut when you are in a relationship?

Chapter 1 Activity

Foster Self-Care: List 5 ways you plan to nurture yourself in the next 30 days. This is especially important when you are going through a tough time in your life (e.g., losses, breakups, big changes). Self-care = Self-love.

Chapter 2 Questions– Lorenzo (Enzo)

1. Is there a particular moment that changed the trajectory of your life?

2. What would you want your spirit guide to be like? Would he be a tough guy like Enzo? Or would she be a glowing angel with a soft voice and gently flapping wings?

3. How would you want your spirit guide to help you?

4. Which former relationship would you absolutely NOT want to revisit and why?

5. Grace really loves her coffee. Which food or drink would you miss most in the afterlife?

Chapter 2 Activity

Create a Spiritual-Abundance Collage: Put on uplifting music and choose pictures that represent how spirituality is present in your life and how it can grow. Spirituality is different for everyone. It could be asking God for help, statements of gratitude, meditation, joining a Bible-study group, connecting with your intuition, or walking in nature. Be creative and have fun!

Chapter 3 Questions– Max and Jesse

1. How were you more fearless or less fearless as a child?

2. Who were your childhood playmates? Are you still in touch?

3. What are your favorite childhood memories? Riding your bike? Roller-skating?

4. What childhood hurt is still with you?

5. What patterns do you see in your relationships that are similar to those from your childhood?

Chapter 3 Activity

Reclaim Your Inner Child: Time travel a bit, and write a letter to your inner child. Tell her/him that you love her/him very much. Communicate that you are here to protect her/him and that you really appreciate who she/he is as a person. That you will honor and respect her/his needs. Then read the letter aloud slowly and notice how you are feeling. It is okay to be sad or cry if you want to. Be real with your emotions, and let them out.

Chapter 4 Questions– Grayson

1. In your life, are there relationships in which you held a grudge? What was the impact of that on you and on others?

2. Have you ever held on to a piece of clothing or some other item from an ex? If yes, what was it? What made you hold on to it? Do you still have it?

3. Which one of your exes would you help and why?

4. How do you think a friend or ex would react if you popped back in as a ghost?

5. How important is date night to a couple?

Chapter 4 Activity

Acknowledge Affirmations of Love: Sit or stand in front of a mirror, and tell yourself, "I am enough." Use other affirmations, such as "I am strong" or "I stand up for myself" or "I am beautiful" or

"I am worthy" or other "I am" statements that are important to you. You can post these phrases where you can see them every day…as friendly reminders!

Chapter 5 Questions- The Closet

1. Have you met or do you know the partner of an ex? How do you get along?

2. When you get ready to go out, for whom do you dress?

3. What do you think about the concept that a partner "completes you"?

4. In what ways do you practice self-care daily?

5. How can you accept your life and be at peace when things are not going according to plan?

Chapter 5 Activity

Clean Out your Closet: Now is the time to go through your closet and remove anything that doesn't make you feel good about yourself. Time to let go of the old and make space for the new!

Chapter 6 Questions- Amy and Grayson

1. Grace was always late when she was alive. Do you show up on time, late, or early? Why do you think that is?

2. In what ways do you think relationships change after the kids come?

3. What patterns do you see in your relationships? Are you always dating the same type of person, meeting them in the same place, or doing the same type of activities?

4. Amy only moved once as a child and disliked being the "new girl." Did your family move around much? Was it difficult for you to be the "new kid"?

5. Grayson completely blows date night by letting work take priority. Has there been a time when you or your partner put work first and damaged your relationship?

Chapter 6 Activity

Plan a Date Night: If you are in a relationship, organize a date night for the two of you. Go to one of your favorite spots. If you are a singleton, take yourself out to a full dinner, not fast food. Get dressed up.

Chapter 7 Questions– Matthew

1. Central Park is Grace's happy place. Where is yours?

2. Grace says, "I never wore my heart on my sleeve or trusted anyone enough to share what was really going on deep down." When have you worn your heart on your sleeve?

3. In which ways can you expand your circle to make sure more champions are in your life?

4. How have your friendships evolved throughout your life?

5. Grace broke Matty's heart on the dance floor. When have you had to tell someone that you didn't feel the same way they did? How did you handle it?

Chapter 7 Activity

Reconnect with Classmates: Get out your high school yearbook. It's time to reminisce. Are you still in contact with any of your classmates? Which ones would it be fun to see again?

Chapter 8 Questions– Nonno Joseph

1. Have your grandparents been a big part of your life? Did or do they live nearby?
2. What is your favorite memory of spending time with your grandparents?
3. How was your relationship with your grandparents different than the one with your parents?
4. Are there other family members who have supported you? Listened to your secrets and concerns?
5. What type of family traditions have you carried on?

Chapter 8 Activity

Assemble a Family-Recipe Collection: Do you have old index cards with family recipes? An old cookbook with handwritten notes? Gather them up, and photocopy them to create a collection you can share with other family members. Old recipes can be photocopied and framed for sentimental family gifts.

Chapter 9 Questions– Hope

1. Who was your best friend growing up and/or in high school? Are you still in touch?

2. Who is your closest friend today? Or do you have a couple? A tribe?

3. How has your best friend supported you through various relationships?

4. What have you told your best friend that you have not told anyone else?

5. Grace and Hope are very different and remained extremely close. In what ways are you and your closest friend alike and different?

Chapter 9 Activity

Bond with Your Bestie: Share this book with your best friend (if you haven't already), and get their feedback to the questions at the end of each chapter.

Chapter 10 Questions- Little Enzo

1. Enzo is quite the character. Have you known anyone like him—gruff on the outside, but a real marshmallow underneath? Do you think Enzo's childhood tragedy makes him a good guide in the afterlife?

2. How has your family impacted the way you love yourself and others?

3. What did you learn about love as a child?

4. How has your upbringing shaped who you are?

5. What relatives who are no longer living would you like to see again and why?

Chapter 10 Activity

Design a Family Tree: Gather pictures, and use either poster board or an online app to create a "tree" with everyone's photos. This is a fun project to share with other family members. Reach out to one family member to whom you haven't spoken in a while.

Chapter 11 Questions- Liam

1. Do you remember your first love? What did you learn from that experience?

2. How was your first encounter with sexual intercourse? What were your expectations? Were they met, or were you disappointed about the experience?

3. Who was the "one who got away" in your life?

4. Have you ever dated someone in whom at first you had no interest? If so, how did your feelings changed along the way?

5. How has love evolved in your relationships? What is important now, as opposed to when you were younger?

Chapter 11 Activity

Write a Valentine to One of Your Great Loves: For this task, include everything you received from this love. Was this the one who introduced you to good wine or food? Did this love share or awaken your love of the outdoors or live music? Use this valentine to celebrate the wins, not the losses of this love. There's no need to send it unless you feel it would be for both parties' highest good. It is more about your acknowledging it for your own growth and development.

Chapter 12 Questions- Liam: Part 2

1. Were you ever brave enough to get your heart broken? If yes, why? If no, why not?

2. What would be the benefit of having others forgive you and of your forgiving others?

3. After one heartbreaking experience, what made you get out there to try again?

4. Have you ever been present when a loved one crossed over?

5. How has that impacted you?

Chapter 12 Activity

Say Goodbye and Forgive with Love. Who are 3 people by whom you were hurt in your life? For each person, say how they hurt you and how you can forgive them. They tried their best; wish them well. Say 5 times, "I forgive you, _(name here)__."

Chapter 13 Questions- Debrief

1. What do you think Grace learned by revisiting her past relationships?

2. What have you learned about yourself in your current and past relationships?

3. As a result of the learning, what will you do differently?

4. What do you need to bring to the light and confront in your life?

5. What needs to happen to change the course of your relationships?

Chapter 13 Activity

Let Go of Limiting Beliefs: Write 3 limiting beliefs on 3 separate pieces of paper. Then take each limiting belief, and burn the paper. Make sure you do it in a place that is safe. Before burning it, rewrite the limiting belief on a new index card, making it into something more positive in nature, something that has the possibility for change and growth.

Limiting belief: "I am never using a dating app again."

Honest and empowering belief: "I am right now taking a break from using the dating app and will check in a few months to see if I am up to trying it again."

OR

Limiting belief: "I am not lovable."

Honest and empowering belief: "Even though I am not in a relationship, I am open to being kind and loving myself during this time."

Chapter 14 Questions- New Beginnings

1. What must you let go of in order to heal and move forward?

2. For what do you need to forgive yourself in your relationships?

3. How can you love yourself more every day?

4. What are you grateful for in your life?

5. How do you, or will you, find your grace within?

Chapter 14 Activity

Write a Positive Prayer or Intention: Using your own words, write a prayer or intention that states that you are firmly and powerfully learning and growing in love. There are limitless possibilities for expanding and transforming into a loving human being. Additionally, share the ways that love is showing up in your life. Flex your gratitude muscle!

Once it is written, read the prayer daily. Keep it alive by vocalizing gratitude for everything in your life that you enjoy and appreciate. Including YOU!

About the Author

C rista Salvatore is a global leadership facilitator, executive coach, and the founder of Spark Truth (www.sprktruth.com). For over fifteen years, her expertise has taught professionals how to tap into their authentic style through increasing self-awareness, leveraging their strengths, and increasing their capacity to take action.

She'd be the first person to admit that she has had her fair share of relationships that have challenged her to the core. Between online dating, matchmakers, setups, and chance encounters, she has certainly experienced love and loss, which lent plenty of inspiration for *The Grace Within*.